ALSO IN THE SERIES

Max Finder Mystery Collected Casebook, Volume 1
2007 Winner for Graphic Novel,
The Association of Educational Publishers'
Distinguished Achievement Award

Max Finder Mystery Collected Casebook, Volume 2
2008 Winner for Graphic Novel,
The Association of Educational Publishers'
Distinguished Achievement Award

Max Finder Mystery Collected Casebook, Volume 3
2008 Finalist for Graphic Novel,
The Association of Educational Publishers'
Distinguished Achievement Award

Max Finder Mystery Collected Casebook, Volume 4

Max Finder Mystery Collected Casebook, Volume 5

Max Finder Mystery Collected Casebook, Volume 6

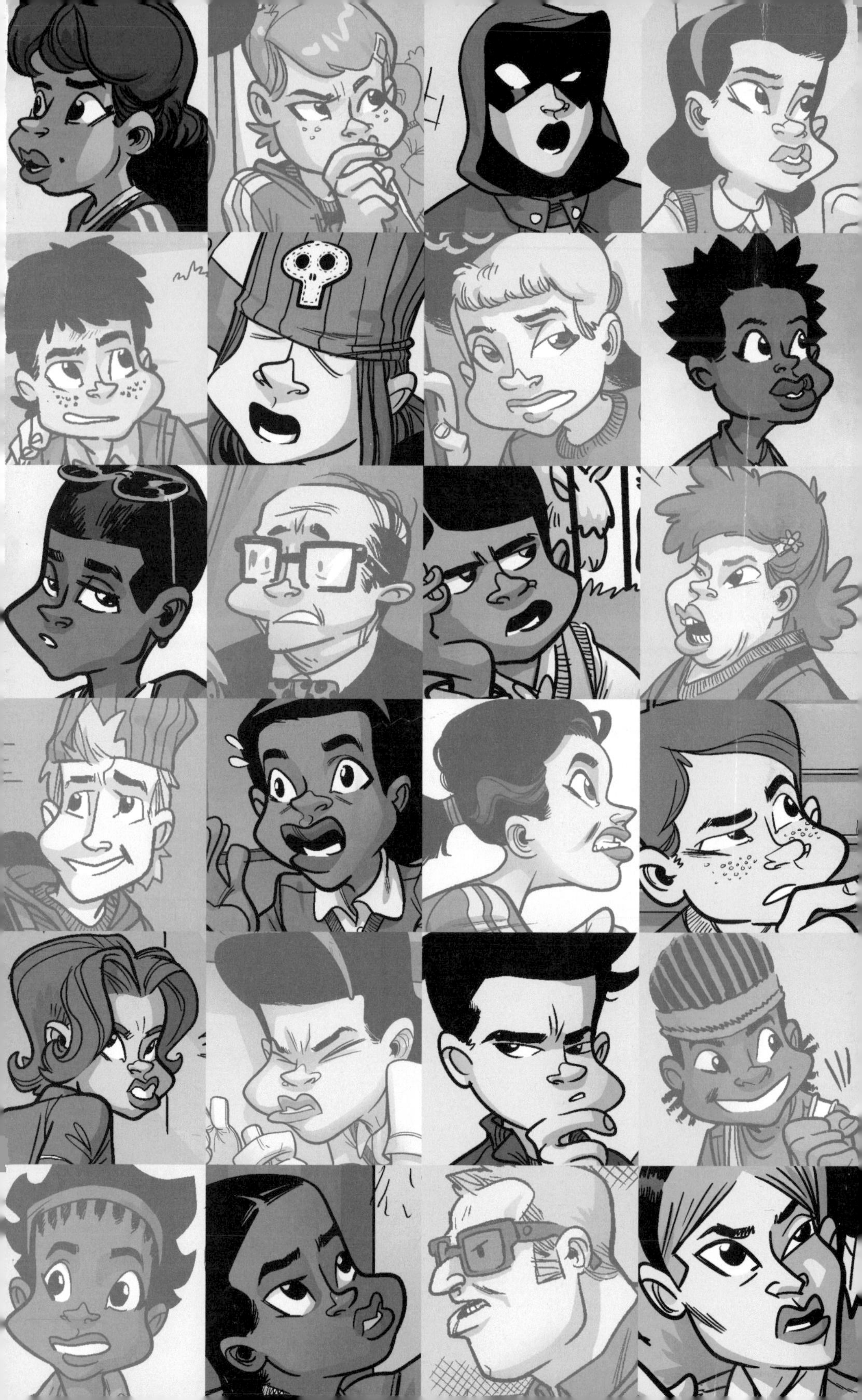

Max Finder MYSTERY

Collected Casebook

Volume 7

Owlkids Books acknowledges the financial support of the Canada Council for the
Arts, the Ontario Arts Council, the Government of Canada through the Canada
Book Fund (CBF) and the Government of Ontario through the Ontario Media
Development Corporation's Book Initiative for our publishing activities.

Published in Canada by
Owlkids Books Inc.
10 Lower Spadina Avenue
Toronto, ON, M5V 2Z2

Published in the United States by
Owlkids Books Inc.
1700 Fourth Street
Berkeley, CA 94710

Library and Archives Canada Cataloguing in Publication

O'Donnell, Liam, 1970-
        Max Finder mystery : collected casebook / Liam O'Donnell, Michael
Cho.

Vol. 6-7 by Craig Battle and Ramón Pérez.
Vol. 5-7 issued also in electronic format.
ISBN 978-1-926973-66-1 (bound : v. 7).--ISBN 978-1-926973-67-8
(pbk. : v. 7)

        1. Detective and mystery comic books, strips, etc. 2. Mystery games.
I. Cho, Michael II. Battle, Craig, 1980- III. Pérez, Ramón IV. Title.

PN6733.O36M38 2006   j741.5'971   C2006-903300-5

Library of Congress Control Number: 2009935531

www.owlkidsbooks.com

Series Design: John Lightfoot/Lightfoot Art & Design Inc.
Design and Art Direction: Caroline Versteeg

Manufactured in Shenzhen, Guangdong, China, in January 2013, by WKT Co. Ltd.
Job #12CB1701

A   B   C   D   E   F

Publisher of Chirp, chickaDEE and OWL
www.owlkidsbooks.com

Max Finder

MYSTERY

Collected Casebook

Volume 7

Craig Battle and Ramón Pérez

Created by Liam O'Donnell

Max Finder Mystery Collected Casebook

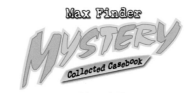

Contents

Stories

Extra Stuff

Collected
Casebook
Volume 7

HEY, MYSTERY BUFFS!

Did you know that the book in your hands features a whopping ten comics and two short stories? Max Finder here, fact collector and junior-high detective. In our hometown of Whispering Meadows, my best friend, Alison, and I are the go-to investigators of mysteries big and small. This casebook collects some of our best moments yet.

From the **Backstage Shakedown** all the way to the **Puzzling Puppet Master**, each mystery is crammed with enough clues, suspects, and red herrings to keep you guessing until the end. We've done all the legwork, but solving the mystery is up to you! Read the mysteries, watch for the clues, and try to crack the case. Solutions are at the end of each comic and story. But remember: real detectives never peek.

So fire up your mystery radar and get solving!

Max

P.S. Check out the lineup on page 11 to get the inside scoop on the characters of Whispering Meadows, and go to page 89 to learn some DIY forensics from my friend Zoe!

CHARACTER LINEUP

WALL

NAME: **MAX FINDER**
@SHERLOCK_FINDER

ACTIVITIES AND INTERESTS:
SOLVING CRIMES, PLAYING
SOCCER, READING THE PAPER

NAME: **ALISON SANTOS**
@NEWSFLASH

ACTIVITIES AND INTERESTS:
PHOTOJOURNALISM,
TRACK TEAM, TRAVELING

NAME: **ZOE PALGRAVE**
@FORENZIC_ZOE

ACTIVITIES AND INTERESTS:
WATCHING FORENSIC SHOWS
IN HER HOME LABORATORY,
SWIMMING

WALL

NAME: MYRON MATTHEWS
@SHADOW_FINDER

ACTIVITIES AND INTERESTS:
STUDYING MAX, PLAYING
SOFTBALL

NAME: JESSICA PEEVES
@THE_JESSICAPEEVES

ACTIVITIES AND INTERESTS:
TRACK TEAM, FASHION,
SLEEPOVERS

NAME: ANA GUZMAN
@GUZMAN_LIGHTNING

ACTIVITIES AND INTERESTS:
HELPING OUT AT HER FAMILY'S
STORE, TRACK AND FIELD

NAME: DOROTHY PAFKO
@KEEPITGREEN

ACTIVITIES AND INTERESTS:
GREEN THUMB CLUB, STUDYING
FOR THE PSATS

CHARACTER LINEUP

NAME: **BEN "BASHER" MCGINTLEY**
@BASHER14

ACTIVITIES AND INTERESTS:
KEEPING MAX AND ALISON OFF HIS BACK, SPORTS

NAME: **JAKE GRANGER**
@JAKE_HOUDINI

ACTIVITIES AND INTERESTS:
HONING HIS MAGIC SKILLS, WRITING

NAME: **CRYSTAL DIALLO**
@CRYSTAL(^_^)

ACTIVITIES AND INTERESTS:
READING AND DRAWING MANGA, WATCHING TV

NAME: **NICHOLAS MUSICCO**
@NICHOLAS_MUSICCO

ACTIVITIES AND INTERESTS:
VOLUNTEERING, WALKING AT SUNRISE

CHARACTER LINEUP

WALL

NAME: **KYLE KRESSMAN**
@GOTCHA

ACTIVITIES AND INTERESTS:
PLAYING PRANKS—LOTS OF PRANKS

NAME: **ALEX RODRIGUEZ**
@ALEX_1

ACTIVITIES AND INTERESTS:
WINNING, SWIMMING, TRIVIA

NAME: **NANDA KANWAR**
@NANDA_BEAR

ACTIVITIES AND INTERESTS:
QUIZ SHOWS, HANGING OUT WITH FRIENDS

NAME: **COURTNEY LeGUIN**
@LEGUINC33

ACTIVITIES AND INTERESTS:
BAKING, GREEN THUMB CLUB, SWIMMING

THE CASE OF THE...

BACKSTAGE SHAKEDOWN

Max Finder, junior-high detective, here. My school's Knowledge Bowl team had won six meets in a row, and we needed to win one more to tie a league record. There was only one problem with that...

WE'RE AT THE HALFWAY MARK OF THE MEET. BAKER HEIGHTS HAS 90 POINTS, WHILE CENTRAL MEADOWS TRAILS WITH 20.

Alex Rodriguez, Dorothy Pafko, and I were getting bowled over by the competition!

My friends Alison and Zoe were in the crowd, along with Donnie Jones, a former Central Meadows student. His team held the record for seven straight wins.

I FEEL SO BAD FOR MAX. DONNIE JONES IS ONE OF HIS HEROES...

I KNOW! IT'S LIKE BAKER HEIGHTS HAS THE ANSWERS BEFORE THE QUESTIONS ARE EVEN ASKED.

THE CATEGORY IS ASTRONOMY. WHICH OF THE FOLLOWING CONSTELLATIONS WAS NOT NAMED FOR SOMETHING IN GREEK MYTHOLOGY? WAS IT...

BUZZ

CORONA AUSTRALIS!

THAT IS CORRECT, MANDEEP... BUT I HADN'T FINISHED THE QUESTION.

UH, I... TOOK A GUESS... OOPS!

Turns out, the piece of paper Mandeep Singh dropped was a sheet with the answers to all of this meet's questions on it. My teammates voiced their anger.

THIS IS A TRAVESTY, MR. LEE! BAKER HEIGHTS SHOULD BE BANNED!

I NEED A FEW MINUTES TO TALK TO THE COACHES. IN THE MEANTIME, CONTESTANTS CAN WAIT BACKSTAGE.

When we got behind the curtains, it was clear by the look on Mandeep's face that he had definitely cheated. It was also clear that his teammates, Stephanie Chang and Jennifer Riley, didn't approve.

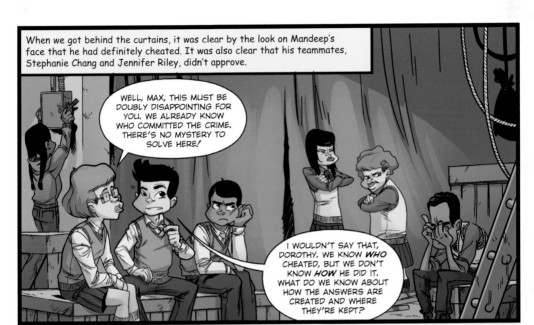

WELL, MAX, THIS MUST BE DOUBLY DISAPPOINTING FOR YOU. WE ALREADY KNOW WHO COMMITTED THE CRIME. THERE'S NO MYSTERY TO SOLVE HERE!

I WOULDN'T SAY THAT, DOROTHY. WE KNOW *WHO* CHEATED, BUT WE DON'T KNOW *HOW* HE DID IT. WHAT DO WE KNOW ABOUT HOW THE ANSWERS ARE CREATED AND WHERE THEY'RE KEPT?

MR. LEE COMES UP WITH THE QUESTIONS THE DAY OF THE MEET. HE INVITES SOMEONE TO HELP HIM, AND THEY ORDER IN FOOD AND WRITE UP THE ANSWERS WHILE THEY EAT LUNCH.

AND THEN HE LOCKS THEM AWAY UNTIL MEET TIME!

THAT MEANS THE ANSWERS NEEDED TO BE STOLEN DURING LUNCH... BUT NONE OF THE BAKER HEIGHTS STUDENTS ARRIVED HERE UNTIL AFTER LAST PERIOD. MANDEEP HAD HELP, AND WE NEED TO FIND OUT WHO PROVIDED IT.

Our next step was to talk to Mandeep, who still seemed to be getting shunned by his teammates.

MANDEEP, WE KNOW YOU COULDN'T HAVE DONE THIS ON YOUR OWN. WHO GAVE YOU THAT CHEAT SHEET?

I DON'T KNOW! THE CHEAT SHEET WAS FOLDED UP ON OUR TEAM'S PODIUM WHEN I ARRIVED.

The paper said "Welcome students of Baker Heights!" on it, and I thought it was a letter or something. By the time I opened it up and saw what it was, I was already in too deep.

IF YOU WANT TO FIND OUT HOW THE CHEAT SHEET GOT THERE, TALK TO NANDA KANWAR. SHE TOLD ME SHE WAS CHEERING FOR US!

Nanda was the stage manager, and she told us that she'd set up the podiums as soon as last period ended. She went backstage to close the curtains, and by the time she came back out, Mr. Lee and Donnie were chatting onstage.

WHAT'S THIS I HEAR ABOUT YOU HOPING BAKER HEIGHTS BEATS THE CENTRAL MEADOWS TEAM?

I'M CHEERING AGAINST ALEX, NOT YOUR TEAM. I OVERHEARD HIM ON THE STAGE AT LUNCH TELLING LESLIE CHANG THAT HE THINKS HE SHOULD BE STAGE MANAGER. WHY DO YOU CARE WHO I CHEER FOR, ANYWAY?

WELL, I'M THINKING SOMEONE HELPED BAKER HEIGHTS CHEAT BY PLANTING THE ANSWERS ON THEIR PODIUM. YOU WERE ONE OF THE FEW WHO HAD ACCESS TO IT.

LESLIE WAS HERE PRACTICING FOR THE SCHOOL PLAY. HER COUSIN STEPHANIE IS ON THE BAKER HEIGHTS TEAM. MAYBE SHE SABOTAGED YOU GUYS TO HELP OUT HER COUSIN.

We tried talking to Leslie's cousin Stephanie, but she wanted nothing to do with us. She and Jennifer said they were in enough trouble already.

WELL, MAX, LOOKS LIKE THERE'S NO ONE LEFT BACKSTAGE TO TALK TO, AND WE CAN'T LEAVE UNTIL MR. LEE COMES BACK.

THAT'S TRUE, BUT I KNOW SOMEONE WHO CAN HELP US OUT. CAN I BORROW YOUR CELL PHONE?

If there's one thing I can count on, it's that Alison and Zoe are always eager to help out with a case.

MAX NEEDS OUR HELP. WE NEED TO FIND LESLIE.

THERE SHE IS! LET'S GO!

OOOFFF!

They'd run into none other than the guest of honor, Donnie Jones. We all knew him from when he used to go to our school, and Alison and Zoe couldn't help but stop and chat.

SORRY YOU DIDN'T GET TO SEE A BETTER MEET, DONNIE.

I FEEL BAD FOR YOU GUYS. THE BONUS ROUND WAS GOING TO HAVE SOME AWESOME QUESTIONS IN IT.

DID YOU SEE ANYTHING ODD WHEN YOU SHOWED UP TO THE MEET?

JUST NANDA AND LESLIE HANGING AROUND THE STAGE. NANDA WOULDN'T LET ANYONE NEAR THE PODIUMS, SO I STAYED OFF THE STAGE ALTOGETHER.

OH, GREAT! NOW LESLIE'S DISAPPEARED, AND MR. LEE'S ON HIS WAY BACK IN. THIS CASE WILL BE A LOT HARDER TO SOLVE ONCE EVERYONE SCATTERS.

DON'T WORRY ABOUT THAT NOW, ZOE. WE'VE JUST GOT TO TEXT MAX ALL WE KNOW.

WELL, THAT WAS NO HELP.

ON THE CONTRARY, DOROTHY!

LC DISAPPEARED! SORRY ABOUT THE MEET. MAX. DJ SAYS BONUS QUESTIONS WERE GREAT.

SORRY FOR MAKING EVERYONE WAIT. WE'VE DECIDED THAT...

HOLD ON, MR. LEE! RIGHT NOW THE CRIME IS MORE IMPORTANT THAN THE PUNISHMENT. I KNOW HOW BAKER HEIGHTS GOT THE CHEAT SHEET.

COACH WHISPERING MEADOWS

BAKER HEIGHTS COACH

Do you know how Baker Heights got the cheat sheet? All the clues are here. Turn the page for the solution.

THE CASE OF THE...
BACKSTAGE SHAKEDOWN

Who gave Baker Heights the cheat sheet at the Knowledge Bowl meet?

Donnie Jones. He wanted to keep his record and gave Baker Heights the cheat sheet so they'd be able to beat Central Meadows.

Clues

- Max poked his head out while Alison was talking to Donnie and noticed that Donnie had a fast-food cup in his hand. Mr. Lee also had a fast-food cup on his podium. This means they ate lunch together.

- Donnie told Alison the bonus questions were going to be awesome. When she relayed this info to Max, he realized that Donnie must've helped Mr. Lee write the answers over lunch.

- Nanda said that Donnie and Mr. Lee were chatting on the stage when she returned from backstage after closing the curtains. That means he would've had an opportunity to drop the cheat sheet off on the Baker Heights podium.

- The cheat sheet was written in red pen. Donnie had a red pen behind his ear when he was talking to Alison and Zoe.

- Alex said Mr. Lee creates the questions and answers for the meet over lunch, but Nanda said Leslie was on the stage at lunch. That means both were far from Mr. Lee's office, and neither could've stolen the answers.

Conclusion

After hearing Max's evidence, Donnie confessed to the crime and Mr. Lee banned him from future Knowledge Bowl events at Central Meadows. Baker Heights got a rematch without Mandeep, who was banned for one meet, and Central Meadows prevailed, tying the record.

THE CASE OF THE...
CREEPY
CUL-DE-SAC

THE CASE OF THE...
CREEPY CUL-DE-SAC

Max Finder, junior-high detective, here. It was after school the day before Halloween, and Alison and I were headed to our friend Crystal Diallo's house on Howell Crescent. She needed our help.

SO, CRYSTAL, YOU THINK YOU'VE GOT A GHOST?

I DON'T KNOW IF IT'S A REAL GHOST, MAX. I JUST KNOW SOMETHING IS SCARING KIDS WHEN THEY WALK DOWN MY STREET.

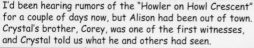

I'd been hearing rumors of the "Howler on Howl Crescent" for a couple of days now, but Alison had been out of town. Crystal's brother, Corey, was one of the first witnesses, and Crystal told us what he and others had seen.

THE SIGHTINGS HAVE HAPPENED RIGHT HERE BETWEEN 3:00 AND 6:00 ON SCHOOL DAYS. WHEN KIDS WALK BY THIS SPOT, THE TREES START TO SHAKE, AND THEY HEAR HOWLING AND CHAINS RATTLING.

A COUPLE OF KIDS THOUGHT IT WAS A PRANK, BUT THERE WAS NOBODY UNDER THE TREE AND NO FOOTPRINTS.

THERE MUST BE A LOGICAL EXPLANATION FOR ALL THIS...

I HOPE SO, MAX. EVERYONE AT SCHOOL THINKS IT'S REAL. NO ONE IS GOING TO COME TO MY FUNHOUSE TOMORROW NIGHT!

Crystal's funhouse was one of the best things about Halloween. But now kids were saying they were afraid to go. I was sure we weren't dealing with a real ghost, but I wasn't sure who to put on our suspect list yet. We went back to Crystal's house so Alison could draw a map of the cul-de-sac.

WITH ALL THE POTENTIAL WITNESSES AROUND, IT WOULD BE IMPOSSIBLE FOR ANYONE TO SNEAK AWAY FROM YOUR STREET WITHOUT BEING SEEN. I THINK THE CULPRIT LIVES RIGHT HERE. AND OUR SUSPECTS ARE...

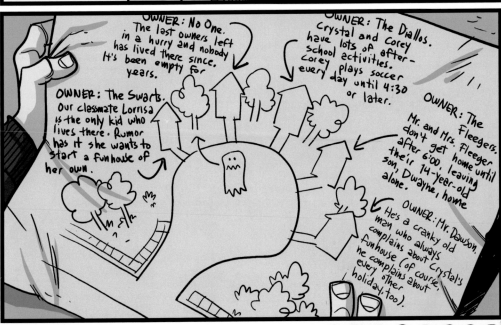

OWNER: No One. The last owners left in a hurry and nobody has lived there since. It's been empty for years.

OWNER: The Diallos. Crystal and Corey have lots of after-school activities. Corey plays soccer every day until 4:30 or later.

OWNER: The Swarts. Our classmate Lorrisa is the only kid who lives there. Rumor has it she wants to start a funhouse of her own.

OWNER: The Fleegers. Mr. and Mrs. Fleeger don't get home until after 6:00, leaving their 14-year-old son, Dwayne, home alone.

OWNER: Mr. Dawson. He's a cranky old man who always complains about Crystal's funhouse (of course, he complains about every other holiday, too).

Now that we'd established suspects, it was time to talk to our witness. Corey is 10 years old, but he and Crystal are very close. He isn't a fan of the funhouse and scares too easily to help out with it.

YOU WERE ONE OF THE FIRST PEOPLE TO ENCOUNTER THE GHOST. CAN YOU TELL US WHAT YOU SAW?

IT'S NOT SO MUCH WHAT I SAW AS WHAT I HEARD...

I was walking home after a rainy soccer practice a few days ago. That's when the tree started to shake, and I heard a chain rattling and a creepy howling noise. I ran home as fast as I could.

LESLIE CHANG CALLED ME AND SAID THE SAME THING. SHE WAS ON HER WAY OVER BUT WAS TOO SCARED AFTER SHE HEARD THE NOISES!

CAN YOU GUYS LEAVE ME ALONE NOW? I'VE GOT HOMEWORK AND I DON'T WANT TO HAVE NIGHTMARES LATER WITH ALL THIS GHOST TALK.

'CLICK'

POOR GUY! HALLOWEEN'S NOT HIS FAVORITE TIME OF YEAR. AND HE MISSES OUT ON SPENDING TIME WITH ME AND MY DAD WHEN WE'RE WORKING ON THE FUNHOUSE.

We left Crystal behind to go talk to her rival, Lorrisa. She didn't deny the fact that she wants to start her own funhouse.

I'M TIRED OF EVERYONE ACTING LIKE CRYSTAL IS THE ONLY ONE ALLOWED TO HAVE FUN ON HALLOWEEN. IS IT SO WRONG TO START A RIVAL FUNHOUSE?

NO, BUT IT'S DEFINITELY WRONG TO SCARE KIDS WHO DON'T WANT TO BE SCARED. CAN WE ASK YOU WHERE YOU'VE BEEN THE LAST FEW DAYS AFTER SCHOOL?

SURE. I'VE GOT NOTHING TO HIDE. I'VE BEEN TUTORING EVERY DAY FOR TWO WEEKS. IN FACT, I JUST GOT HOME. NOW IF YOU'LL EXCUSE ME, I HAVE MY OWN HOMEWORK TO DO.

DO YOU BELIEVE HER, MAX?

I DON'T KNOW, ALISON. LORRISA GETS GOOD GRADES, SO SHE'D MAKE A GOOD TUTOR. FUNNY THAT SHE DIDN'T TELL US WHO SHE'S TUTORING, THOUGH...

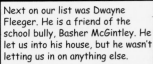Next on our list was Dwayne Fleeger. He is a friend of the school bully, Basher McGintley. He let us into his house, but he wasn't letting us in on anything else.

YOU AND YOUR BUDDY BASHER LIKE MESSING WITH KIDS, DON'T YOU, DWAYNE?

YEAH... I MEAN, NO! IF YOU'RE TALKING ABOUT THE HOWLER, I HAVE NOTHING TO DO WITH THAT.

HOW CAN WE BE SURE? WHAT HAVE YOU BEEN DOING AFTER SCHOOL OTHER THAN PLAYING VIDEO GAMES SOLO?

NONE OF YOUR BUSINESS, DORK-TECTIVES! I DON'T HAVE TO TELL YOU ANYTHING. HOW ABOUT YOU GUYS GET LOST?

OKAY, FINE, LET'S GO... MAX?!

Alison wasn't impressed with my work ethic, but she did get us outside just in time.

LOOK, MAX! THE HOWLER HAS STRUCK AGAIN!

AND THERE'S MR. DAWSON.

THAT'S RIGHT, YOU KIDS! DON'T COME BACK NOW, YOU HEAR?!

AIEEEEEEEEEEE

EEEEEE

COME ON, MAX. THE TREE IS STILL SHAKING. LET'S GO LOOK UNDER IT FOR CLUES.

NO NEED, ALISON. I KNOW WHO THE HOWLER IS.

Do you know who's creeping out kids on Howell Crescent? All the clues are here. Turn the page for the solution.

THE CASE OF THE...
CREEPY CUL-DE-SAC

Who was doing the howling on Howell Crescent?

Corey Diallo. He was jealous of the amount of time Crystal got to spend with their dad, so he tried to sabotage the funhouse by scaring away potential visitors.

Clues

- When the two girls were scared off, Max saw a ladder leaning up against the side of the balcony on the second floor of the empty house. Earlier it was up against the side of the Diallos' house and leaning into Corey's room. That's how he shook the tree without being seen underneath it.

- Crystal said her brother plays soccer every day after school, but the soccer cleats on his floor were clean as new. He was skipping soccer practice to scare kids and then hiding on the deck of the empty house.

- Dwayne had a chain around his neck, but it was too small to make a noise anyone would hear. The chain sound everyone heard was made by the hanging planter on the balcony of the empty house. It was hanging from chains.

- Max noticed a practice quiz on the coffee table at Dwayne's house. It was graded and signed by Lorrisa.

That means Lorrisa was tutoring Dwayne after school. Dwayne didn't want to admit it to Max or Alison because caring about his grades would ruin his tough-guy image.

- Lorrisa would need kids to come down the street to have a successful funhouse. Max knew she wouldn't sabotage Crystal by scaring kids away because she'd be sabotaging herself in the process.

- Mr. Dawson may have wanted the kids to go away and stop making so much noise, but he wasn't the Howler. He was on his lawn across the street from the empty house when the tree started shaking and scared the girls away.

Conclusion

When Max and Alison went looking for Corey, he was hiding behind the empty house. He confessed and apologized to his sister, who forgave him. Both funhouses were great successes, and everyone, even Corey, had a frightfully good time.

THE CASE OF THE...
BAFFLING BAKE-OFF

THE CASE OF THE...
BAFFLING BAKE-OFF

Max Finder, junior-high detective, here. Five kids from our school were competing in a bake-off for charity at Gander Banks Park, so Alison, Zoe, and I had to check it out.

WELCOME TO THE BAKE-OFF ON THE BANKS!

COME GET A TREAT AND SEE — SKYSCRAPER SAM!

ANIMAL FARM

JEFF COLEMAN CARAMEL NUT-FUDGE

WELCOME TO THE BAKE-OFF ON THE BANKS, YOU GUYS!

COURTNEY LEGUIN BANANA-CHOCOLATE MUFFINS!

URSULA CURTIS PUMPKIN TARTS

ALEX RODRIGUEZ DATE SQUARES

ANA GUZMAN oatmeal+raisin COOKIES!

Ursula Curtis is the organizer of the event. She set it up so that each kid charges one dollar per treat. Whoever makes the most money will be declared the winner and will get to pick which charity the donation goes to.

ANA
JEFF
COURTNEY
URSULA
ALEX

WE'VE RAISED MORE THAN $200 SO FAR! LAST TIME I CHECKED EVERYONE'S INDIVIDUAL CASH BOXES, COURTNEY LEGUIN WAS IN THE LEAD WITH $55.

I CAN SEE WHY. BANANA-CHOCOLATE MUFFINS ARE MY FAVORITE!

Speaking of Courtney...

STEP RIGHT UP AND GRAB A MUFFIN, EVERYONE! ALL PROCEEDS GO TO CHARITY!

28

Over the screeching of Courtney's megaphone, Ursula said she rented a giant costume of cartoon character Skyscraper Sam so they could hand out balloons and draw people's attention to the event.

I GOT NICHOLAS MUSICCO TO DRESS UP IN THE OUTFIT. IT'S MAINLY FOR THE LITTLE KIDS, BUT ALL THE BAKERS WERE REALLY EXCITED ABOUT IT—ESPECIALLY ALEX RODRIGUEZ.

URSULA! THE SKYSCRAPER SAM COSTUME IS MISSING!

Nicholas told us he took the costume off to get a breath of fresh air. Then it disappeared.

THE HEAD OF THE COSTUME IS SO TIGHT I CAN'T WEAR IT FOR TOO LONG. SO I TOOK IT OFF, AND NOW URSULA'S GOING TO LOSE HER $50 DEPOSIT. IT'S ALL MY FAULT!

DON'T WORRY, NICHOLAS. BEFORE LONG WE'LL HAVE...

FOUND IT!

Well, that was easy! Ursula found the costume in a secluded spot behind a trash can and decided to hang on to it for the rest of the day. After all the commotion had died down, Courtney noticed something distressing: her cash box was missing now, too.

IT WAS RIGHT HERE A FEW MINUTES AGO! I HAD $62 IN THERE!

HOLD ON, COURTNEY. TELL US EVERYTHING YOU REMEMBER ABOUT THE LAST TIME YOU SAW IT.

I was selling lots of muffins right up until 3:30. That's when Nicholas came by in the Skyscraper Sam costume and distracted me. At least he gave me a balloon!

I DON'T REMEMBER SEEING MY CASHBOX SINCE THEN. A COUPLE OF MINUTES AFTER THAT, NICHOLAS RAN BY SHOUTING THAT THE COSTUME HAD BEEN STOLEN. YOU DON'T THINK HE HAD ANYTHING TO DO WITH THIS, DO YOU?

I DON'T KNOW. IT'S POSSIBLE HE LOST THE COSTUME ON PURPOSE TO CREATE A DIVERSION. EITHER WAY, WE'D BETTER HAVE ANOTHER CHAT WITH HIM.

Before we left, Zoe found small traces of grayish-blue costume foam on Courtney's table, confirming that Nicholas had got close enough to steal the cash box. But Alison had another theory.

IF COURTNEY'S TELLING THE TRUTH, THE *$62* SHE RAISED WOULD MAKE HER THE CLEAR WINNER OF THE BAKE-OFF. BUT IF NOT, MAYBE ONE OF THE OTHERS PASSED HER TOTAL. SHE COULD'VE HIDDEN THE BOX TO COLLECT THE CASH AND THE PRIZE AT THE SAME TIME.

PETT
ZOO

We found Nicholas sitting under a tree by the park's animal farm. He was still sulking about the disappearing costume.

I'M GLAD URSULA FOUND IT, BUT IT'S SO STRANGE. AFTER I TOOK OFF THE COSTUME I LEFT IT RIGHT HERE. THEN I WENT TO GRAB A TREAT, BUT BY THE TIME I GOT BACK IT WAS GONE.

WHAT HAPPENED RIGHT BEFORE THAT? COURTNEY SAYS YOU DROPPED BY HER TABLE AT *3:30* AND GAVE HER A BALLOON.

THERE'S NO WAY I COULD HAVE GIVEN HER A BALLOON. I RAN OUT OF THEM AROUND *2:30.* BESIDES, I DIDN'T GO BY COURTNEY'S TABLE ALL DAY! THE TREAT I GRABBED WAS FROM ALEX RODRIGUEZ'S TABLE. I DON'T KNOW WHY, BUT HE WAS SITTING THERE FUMING.

Alex is one of the most competitive kids at our school. But when we found him at his table, he sure wasn't enjoying the competition.

WHAT'S WRONG, ALEX?

WHAT'S WRONG IS NO ONE'S BUYING MY DATE SQUARES! I'VE SOLD HALF AS MANY TREATS AS EVERYONE ELSE, AND YET I FOLLOWED THE RECIPE TO THE MILLIGRAM OF INGREDIENT AND MINUTE OF BAKING TIME.

ALEX RODRIGUEZ
DATE SQUARES

AND NOT ONLY AM I NOT SELLING ANYTHING, BUT I HAVE TO LISTEN TO CARLA BAXTER COME OVER HERE EVERY FIVE MINUTES TO COMPLAIN ABOUT ALL THE NOISE COURTNEY IS MAKING WITH HER MEGAPHONE.

BUT I'LL HAVE THE LAST LAUGH TODAY. TRUST ME!

Carla Baxter is a student at Whispering Meadows High and a volunteer at the park's animal farm. The zoo has fallen on hard times recently, but it used to be one of the most popular parts of the park.

WE HEARD YOU WERE OVER AT THE BAKE-OFF A FEW TIMES THIS AFTERNOON. DID YOU SEE ANYONE WHO COULD'VE STOLEN A CASH BOX?

WHERE GOES NICHOLAS?

IF YOU'RE OVER HERE, THEN... *STOP THAT SKYSCRAPER!*

NO, SORRY, YOU GUYS. I JUST DROPPED BY BECAUSE THAT MEGAPHONE WAS GETTING TOO LOUD.

CHOMP CHOMP

HEY, LOOK. THERE GOES NICHOLAS.

GOTCHA!

HEY!

ALEX?!

DO YOU MIND TELLING US WHAT YOU'RE DOING IN THIS COSTUME?

HE STOLE IT! HE PROBABLY TOOK THE CASH BOX, TOO!

NO, I... I JUST WANTED TO TRY IT ON!

SAVE IT, ALEX. I KNOW WHO STOLE COURTNEY'S CASH BOX.

Do you know who stole the cash box? All the clues are here. Turn the page for the solution.

THE CASE OF THE...
BAFFLING BAKE-OFF

Who stole the cash box?

Carla Baxter. She was tired of Courtney's megaphone noise, so she stole her cash box to end the bake-off early—and get some money for the animal farm.

Clues

- Courtney said Nicholas gave her a balloon right around the time the cash box was stolen, but she didn't know this for sure. Also, when Max and Alison first arrived at the bake-off, Alison saw both Nicholas and Skyscraper Sam walking around at the same time. Therefore, someone other than Nicholas was wearing the costume.

- The costume was placed near the animal farm when Nicholas took it off, giving Carla easy access to it.

- Nicholas said the head of the costume was really tight, and he had the red mark on his forehead to show for it. Alison noticed that Carla had a similar red mark.

- Max noticed that Courtney's balloon had a picture of an alpaca on it. He noticed the same type of balloon later at the animal farm, which Carla had easy access to.

- Ursula said Alex was especially excited about the Skyscraper Sam costume. He borrowed it from Ursula in the end to cheer himself up after finishing last in the bake-off. Alex couldn't have been the one to steal it in the first place because Nicholas was buying a treat from him at the time it went missing.

Conclusion

When Max and Alison presented their evidence, Carla confessed and returned the cash box. In turn, Courtney apologized for upsetting people with her megaphone noise. She never realized it was bothering people, and Alex was too preoccupied to tell Courtney that Carla was annoyed. In the end, Courtney was declared the winner and chose to give the money they raised to a very worthy cause: the animal farm.

The Case of the
Icy Incident
As told by Alison Santos

"Okay, freeze!" I yelled, my breath hanging in the air. "Stop right there!"

Layne Jennings was standing in front of me. I could tell she was getting ready to bolt, but I wasn't about to let that happen.

"And...gotcha!"

As I snapped my last picture of the night, Layne exhaled loudly and slumped over at the waist, pretending to pass out, her hands brushing the snowy ground beneath her feet.

"Please tell me you got it that time," she said. "I can't pose for another of those. Even my ice sculpture is getting tired!"

I was on assignment for my school newspaper at the Great Valley Ice Sculpture Competition in Twindale, only a short bus ride from Whispering Meadows. The event had been held outdoors in the dead of winter for years, but this was the first time organizers were opening it up to anyone under 18, and Layne, one of our school's best artists, decided to enter.

"I got it, I got it," I said. "Just tell me about your piece and we're done."

The sculpture was taller than Layne herself. It was of a killer whale leaping out of the snowy ground the way real killer whales leap out of water, and according to Layne anyway, it had a great chance of winning the top prize in the youth division. She told me that balancing the sculpture on the killer whale's tail was the hardest part and would earn her big points from the judges.

"Who's your main competition?" I asked, flipping the page on my reporter's notepad.

"George Givens," Layne said coldly. "He's the son of the organizer of the event, and he's been carving ice sculptures longer than any other kid in the competition. He's got lots of talent...and lots of attitude. His sculpture is over there somewhere."

Layne pointed aimlessly out across the snowy park space in the general direction of several other ice sculptures. It was nearly 9:00 p.m., only a few other artists were still working, and Layne was far too tired to give me an up-close look at George's creation. I took the hint and started packing up my camera and notepad.

"All right, then! See you tomorrow?" I said.

"Good song," I thought as I stirred awake the next morning. I was practically nodding my head to the beat before I realized it was the ringtone on my cell phone.

"Hello?" I croaked into the receiver as I squinted at my alarm clock. It was 7:15 a.m.

"Alison!" Layne screamed in my ear. "I'm at the competition. You have to get here now! Someone's stolen my sculpture, and there's no time to make another one before judging!"

These are the moments when you're happy your best friend is a junior-high detective. Sadly, these are also the moments when you're angry your best friend, the junior-high detective, has a large extended family and is out of town visiting someone. But this mystery couldn't wait for Max. I threw on some clothes, called my friend and forensics expert, Zoe, and hopped on a bus for Twindale.

Zoe met me at the park gates, forensics kit in hand. "What's the story?" she asked as we walked toward Layne's carving area. I told her about the sculpture and what Layne had said, even though I couldn't believe it was stolen.

"That thing must've weighed a ton...."

Zoe said it was possible someone with a truck and a pulley system could've lifted it up and carried it away—Layne's area was right next to the park's parking lot, after all.

Layne was waiting anxiously by her site. But where her sculpture used to be, there was a round patch of frozen grass. The snow around it was slick, smooth, and shiny.

"The sculpture wasn't stolen," Zoe declared immediately. "It was destroyed. Melted, to be exact."

"But that's crazy," Layne said. "It's freezing out here!"

"Whoever did this wasn't relying on Mother Nature, Layne. They used a heat source of some sort."

Before Zoe could take the theory any further, Mr. Givens, the event organizer, showed up in a huff with his son, George, in tow. The family resemblance was clear—both were tall and slim with slicked-back black hair. Between shouts into a walkie-talkie, Mr. Givens told us he'd heard that something had been stolen and came by to check it out.

"But what's the crime here?" George said skeptically. "I don't see anything."

"How about destruction of private...ice!" Zoe shouted.

With one hand on Zoe's shoulder to calm her down, I used the other to grab my digital camera and scroll through the photos I took the day before. Mr. Givens seemed genuinely impressed...if a little bit distracted.

"That's a nice sculpture," he said. "Are you sure you're in the right spot?"

"Yes, Mr. Givens, I—" Layne started to say, but a squawk from Mr. Givens's walkie-talkie interrupted her.

"I'm sorry, Layne," he said, "but I have to run. I'm sure it'll turn up. Good luck in the contest!"

Despite our protests, Mr. Givens and his sneering son hurried away. Zoe set to work combing the crime scene for further clues. She quickly determined that the culprit must've committed the crime overnight, when few people were around. That worked with our timeline, as Layne and I left the site at 9:30 p.m., and Layne returned at 7:00 a.m. When I asked Zoe about the heat source she had mentioned, she had a quick answer.

"My guess is a hair dryer," she said.

"Would that be strong enough?" I asked.

"It could be. If the culprit had enough time."

"But hair dryers don't run on batteries," Layne countered. "How could someone have used one in the middle of a field?"

And that's when I put my own observational skills to work. I could clearly make out, among the many indistinguishable footprints in the snow, a thin, wavy line leading away from the grassy patch.

"That's how," I said. "Someone used an extension cord to get the hair dryer out here, and we're going to use it to lead us right back to them."

The line in the snow led us all the way to an outlet on the side of a small, plain brick building in the middle of the park, confirming my suspicions about the extension cord. Layne told us it was a storage building as well as the office of the park caretaker, Mimi Carson. Mimi was on record saying the competition was bad for the park.

"Can I help you kids with something?" Mimi said, poking her head out the door of the building. She was wearing a dark green coat with wet shoulders over blue overalls. The corners of her boots were crusted with ice, and she had fir needles in her bouncy, wavy blond hair.

"Hi...Mimi, is it?" I said. "We're investigating a crime. Can we come in?"

Mimi led us to the inside of the building, which was toasty warm and comfortable—exactly the opposite of outside. Despite all the random equipment and paperwork lying around, Mimi treated the space like a second home. As she served us tea and cookies, she apologized for her sodden appearance. She had been knocking some heavy snow off trees in the park to ease the burden on the branches and got a little soaked. She told us she passed by us the night before, when we were taking pictures for the newspaper. She seemed outraged that someone would steal the killer whale sculpture.

"That's interesting. We heard you weren't a fan of the sculptures," Zoe said.

"The sculptures I love. The competition I don't. The park grounds don't stand up well to all the extra foot traffic—or the litter people leave lying around after they're done looking at the art. It makes it really tough to clean things up come springtime. I just wish they'd host the competition somewhere else, is all."

"Would you happen to have an extension cord we could look at?" I asked her.

"I'm sorry. I do, but it died on me just the other day. I think Mr. Givens might have some spares, though."

After we left, we walked off in search of George, and Zoe asked me if I thought Mimi had anything to do with the theft.

"I don't know. She certainly has a strong motive."

"If she did it, why would she choose Layne's sculpture over all the others? It's not like she's the most famous entrant or anything."

"Not yet, anyway," Layne said, smiling.

Despite her surprisingly resilient mood, Layne had no interest in coming with us to talk to George, so she went back to her area to see if she could get any info from her carving neighbors. Zoe and I, meanwhile, got a quick look at the rest of the entries in the contest: there were sculptures of famous people, mythical creatures, abstract objects...you name it. George had created one of the most impressive of all. It was of a hockey goalie making a glove save in front of a net.

"Cool sculpture, George," I said, sneaking up on him as he brushed ice fragments off his sculpture with a rag. "Shame that it would be disqualified if we found out you melted Layne's sculpture."

As George snorted and stuffed the rag into a backpack full of tools, we told him the sculpture had been destroyed overnight and asked him about his whereabouts.

"Okay, okay," he said. "It's no secret I want to win this thing, and I'm jealous of the fact that Layne has a reporter following her around, but I wasn't even here overnight. I got a ride home with my dad at 10:00 or so. How was I supposed to melt a sculpture while I was asleep?"

"If you weren't here, do you know who might've been?" Zoe asked.

"Normally the park security guard is here all night, but my dad told me he went home sick yesterday," George said. "The only one I can think of who would've been here is Sandra Smalls. She's my neighbor and is entered in the adult category. She prefers to work at night instead of during the day."

We looked where he was pointing, and I immediately started to rethink our theory that the killer whale sculpture had been melted. That's because it seemed to be sitting right in the middle of Sandra Smalls's area. As Zoe and I crept closer, however, we started noticing differences—bigger eyes, smaller fin, and more teeth in the mouth. We were still amazed at how similar the two sculptures were, though.

"She's a beauty, isn't she?" said Sandra, a slim older woman with funky glasses, tie-dyed clothing, and a shock of gray hair sticking out underneath her toque. She was chipping a small piece of ice away from the killer whale's mouth with what looked like a large screwdriver.

"Yes, it is. It's very similar to one we saw on the other side of the park," I said. "Do you know Layne Jennings?"

The blood drained from Sandra's face. "Someone else is carving a killer whale sculpture?"

Once again I grabbed my camera and pulled up the pictures. Sandra's face went from stark white to beet red. "She copied my idea! If I get my way, that sculpture will never see the light of day! I'm going to talk to Mr. Givens about this."

It was nearing judging time as Sandra ran off to find Mr. Givens, practically tripping on the bright-orange cord trailing behind Mimi, who was hooking up a loudspeaker for the awards ceremony. That's when Layne came running over with some news.

"I just got a hot tip from another competitor. He said he saw George Givens walking near my area with a backpack last night just after I left. Maybe he had a hair dryer in the backpack!"

"Maybe, Layne," I said, a knowing grin coming over my face. "But I think I'm ready to catch the slippery saboteur."

Do you know who melted the ice sculpture?
Turn the page for the solution.

THE CASE OF THE...
ICY INCIDENT

Who melted Layne's ice sculpture?

Mimi Carson.

Clues

- Mimi said she didn't have an extension cord, but Alison noticed that she was using a bright-orange one when hooking up the loudspeaker. She lied to make herself look innocent.

- Mimi said she saw Alison taking photographs for the paper the night the sculpture was melted. That explains why she chose Layne's sculpture to melt. She knew that Layne had a reporter following her around, and that news about the vandalism would get out into the world, hopefully spelling the end of the ice sculpture contest.

- Mimi apologized for her sodden appearance, and yet Alison described her hair as bouncy. That means she dried her hair in between knocking snow off the trees and talking with the detectives. Alison knew she must have a hair dryer.

- George said he got a ride home with his dad at around 10:00 p.m., which explains why he was near Layne's spot just after she left at 9:30 p.m. As Alison noted, Layne's area was close to the parking lot. As Alison also noted, his backpack was full of tools—not hair dryers.

- Sandra wanted to get Layne's sculpture removed from the competition—that means she thought it was still around. Alison said Layne's sculpture was on the other side of the park, which means that Sandra was unlikely to have come across it.

Conclusion

When Alison presented her evidence to Mr. Givens, he confronted Mimi. She confessed and apologized for her behavior, vowing to embrace future editions of the competition. Upon hearing Alison's evidence, Mr. Givens allowed Layne to enter Alison's photos of her sculpture in the competition. Along with George, she won a gold medal—one of very few handed out at the entire competition.

THE CASE OF THE...
SNIPPY SKI TRIP

THE CASE OF THE...
SNIPPY SKI TRIP

Max Finder, junior-high detective, here. Alison and I were hitting the slopes Saturday morning at Whispering Mountain. It was the first run of the day, and we were already in top form. At least I was.

COME ON, ALISON! HURRY!

NICE RUN, ALISON! YOU ALMOST GOT ME THAT TIME.

NICE TRY, MAX. I BEAT YOU BY A MILE.

After much debate, we called it a draw and went over to visit our friend Zoe, who was taking part in a beginners' class that morning. Or so we thought.

MAX! ALISON! SOMEONE SABOTAGED THE ROPE TOW!

Rope tows pull people up from the bottom of ski runs. The rope on this one had been severed, and Zoe's class was canceled because of it. She suspected foul play.

I HEARD THAT THE SKI CLUB IS ALWAYS COMPLAINING ABOUT THIS TOW. MAYBE THAT OLD ROPE FINALLY JUST SNAPPED FROM THE CONSTANT PULLING.

WHEN ROPES SNAP, THEY HAVE FRAYED EDGES. THE ENDS OF THIS ROPE ARE CUT STRAIGHT ACROSS. BESIDES, THE MACHINE HADN'T EVEN BEEN TURNED ON YET. SOMEONE WANTED THE ROPE TOW OUT OF COMMISSION.

The ski club's maintenance worker, Mr. Sheffield, checks all the lifts starting at 8:00 a.m. Just before the hill opened at 9:00 a.m., he noticed that the rope tow was sabotaged.

THERE ARE SKI BOOT TREADS ALL AROUND THIS SPOT, AND THEY SEEM FRESH. IT'S *9:15* A.M. NOW. I'M GUESSING THIS COULDN'T HAVE HAPPENED MORE THAN AN HOUR AGO.

WHY WOULD SOMEONE HIT THE HILL EARLY TO CUT A ROPE TOW LINE?

WE MIGHT NOT KNOW THE MOTIVE, BUT WE DO HAVE THE FIRST EXHIBIT FOR OUR CASE FILE. LOOK!

We found Mr. Sheffield hanging a "Closed" sign at the maintenance shed. He recognized the shears immediately.

WE FOUND THEM DOWN BY THE SPOT WHERE THE ROPE WAS CUT. ANY IDEA HOW THEY GOT THERE?

BE CAREFUL WITH THOSE! WHERE DID YOU GET THEM?

NONE, AND I DON'T CARE! THERE'S ALWAYS SOMETHING BREAKING DOWN ON THIS ROPE TOW, AND I'LL BE HAPPY TO SEE IT GONE.

WHAT DO YOU MEAN? WHERE'S IT GOING?

THE ROPE TOW'S GETTING REPLACED AT THE END OF THE SEASON. AND SOME PEOPLE, LIKE MRS. PRICE OVER THERE, THINK THAT'S NOT SOON ENOUGH.

FINALLY! I'M SO GLAD THAT ROPE IS OUT OF COMMISSION!

The ecstatic skier was Mrs. Price, the mother of our classmate Sasha, and one of the richest women in town. Alison and I decided to leave Zoe at the chalet and tail Mrs. Price to the top of the hill.

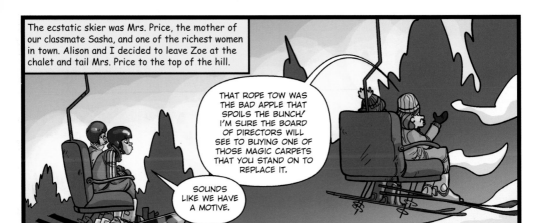

THAT ROPE TOW WAS THE BAD APPLE THAT SPOILS THE BUNCH! I'M SURE THE BOARD OF DIRECTORS WILL SEE TO BUYING ONE OF THOSE MAGIC CARPETS THAT YOU STAND ON TO REPLACE IT.

SOUNDS LIKE WE HAVE A MOTIVE.

As we hopped off the chairlift, we were distracted from our task. It was clear our friend Ethan Webster needed our help.

WHOA! LOOK OUT BELOW!

ETHAN! ARE YOU ALL RIGHT?

LOOKS LIKE YOU'D BETTER STICK TO THE BASKETBALL COURT, ETHAN!

After we hiked up the hill, Ethan filled us in on his hecklers. Turns out James Tiberius had told him basketball players weren't real athletes and challenged him to a race.

JAMES'S FAMILY HAS A HOUSE UP HERE. THEY COME UP EVERY FRIDAY NIGHT AND STAY UNTIL MONDAY MORNING. HE SNOWBOARDS ALL THE TIME.

AND, UH, YOU DON'T.

I KNOW, BUT HE SEEMED REALLY SURPRISED WHEN I ACCEPTED THE CHALLENGE. I THINK HE'S WORRIED I'LL BE GOOD WHEN I GET GOING. WHEN THE BUNNY HILL GOT CLOSED DOWN, I HAD TO COME UP HERE.

YOU WERE ON THE BUNNY HILL THIS MORNING?

YEAH. I REALLY WANTED TO TAKE THE BEGINNERS' CLASS, BUT SOME OTHER PEOPLE SEEMED HAPPY IT WAS CANCELED. SASHA PRICE WAS ONE OF THEM.

We found both Zoe and Sasha Price in the chalet. I don't think Sasha was expecting us.

MIND IF WE HAVE A WORD?

HEY, SASHA!

SORRY ABOUT THAT. WE JUST WANT TO KNOW WHAT YOU HAVE AGAINST THE BEGINNERS' CLASS YOU'RE TAKING. ETHAN WEBSTER SAYS YOU DIDN'T WANT TO BE THERE.

ETHAN'S RIGHT! MY MOM WANTS ME TO TAKE THAT CLASS. THE ONLY THING SHE HATES MORE THAN THAT ROPE TOW DOWN THERE IS THE FACT THAT I DON'T LIKE SKIING.

HEY, LOOK! IT'S ETHAN. YOU MIGHT NOT RECOGNIZE HIM WITH HIS HEAD OUT OF THE SNOW!

THOSE GUYS ARE GETTING ON MY NERVES.

TELL ME ABOUT IT! JAMES'S FRIENDS CAME UP HERE ON THE SHUTTLE BUS WITH ME. THEY WERE SO ANNOYING, I THOUGHT SASHA WAS GOING TO STRANGLE THEM!

WHAT TIME DID YOUR BUS GET HERE?

ABOUT 9:00 A.M. WHY?

WE KNOW WHO SABOTAGED THE ROPE TOW. AND THEY'RE IN THIS CHALET.

BECAUSE THAT TIMING IS THE KEY TO THIS.

Do you know who sabotaged the rope tow? All the clues are here. Turn the page for the solution.

THE CASE OF THE...
SNIPPY SKI TRIP

Who cut the rope tow?

James Tiberius. He was worried Ethan would beat him in a race if he got the chance to learn how to ski, so he sabotaged the bunny hill and the beginners' class.

Clues

- As Max, Alison, and Zoe talked to Mr. Sheffield, Max saw that the window of the maintenance shed was open, and that snow had been knocked off the sill. That means someone with knowledge of Mr. Sheffield's schedule climbed into the shed to steal the hedge shears. As Alison noted, James is a regular at the ski hill and would know the schedule, especially for the weekends.

- Max noticed a nail sticking up on the sill of the maintenance shack with a little white stuffing stuck to it. When he saw James at the chalet, he noticed that James's snow pants had a rip in the knee and stuffing was sticking out. That means James was the one who broke into the shed.

- Mr. Sheffield discovered that the rope tow was damaged before the hills opened. That means none of the kids on the shuttle bus, including Sasha and James's two friends, could have done it.

- Zoe said she found ski boot treads around the spot where the rope was cut. But Mr. Sheffield was wearing regular winter boots with chunky treads. He didn't get close enough to the rope that morning to cut it.

- Sasha said the only thing her mom hates more than the rope tow is the fact that she doesn't like to ski, but Sasha couldn't take the beginners' class without the rope tow. That means Mrs. Price wouldn't have been the one to cut the rope.

Conclusion

After Max and Alison presented their evidence, James confessed. He told them he had a lot of respect for Ethan's athleticism and didn't want to get embarrassed at his best sport. He apologized to Ethan and promised to help him learn to snowboard. He also donated six months' allowance to replace the rope on the tow.

THE CASE OF THE...
MATH CLUB CONUNDRUM

Max Finder, junior-high detective, here. We were at school early so Alison could take photos of the math club's maze contest. Our friend Stuart DeSilva was in the club and up for the challenge.

THANKS FOR COMING WITH ME, YOU GUYS. WHOEVER FINISHES THE MAZE IN THE SHORTEST TIME GETS TO BE CLUB PRESIDENT.

NO PROBLEM, STUART. THE PHOTOS I GET WILL MAKE A GREAT ADDITION TO THIS WEEK'S ISSUE OF THE *METEOR*.

THAT'S TRUE, ALISON, BUT COULDN'T YOU HAVE MADE ANY SUBTRACTIONS FROM ALL THIS CAMERA EQUIPMENT?

MR. REED SAID HE'D BE HERE AT 7:30 A.M. SO POTENTIAL CANDIDATES COULD START TAKING THE TEST. I JUST WANTED TO BE THE FIRST PERSON... HERE?!

DONE!

BEEP

INCREDIBLE, DOROTHY! ONE MINUTE AND 13 SECONDS! I HAD ESTIMATED AT LEAST FIVE MINUTES PER PERSON!

After Mr. Reed erased Dorothy's lines in the maze, he gave the chalk to Stuart. He's one of the best math students in school, and he was determined to give Dorothy a run for her money...

FOUR MINUTES AND THIRTY SECONDS FLAT! GOOD TIME, STUART.

BEEP

But not good enough. Dorothy beat him by a full three minutes.

Outside, Stuart wasn't taking his defeat well.

IT'S NOT POSSIBLE. I'VE BEEN STUDYING MAZE CONSTRUCTION FOR A WEEK. DOROTHY MUST'VE CHEATED TO GET A TIME LIKE THAT!

HOLD ON, STUART. THAT ISN'T FAIR. YOU DON'T HAVE ANY PROOF. ARE YOU SURE YOU'RE NOT JUST JEALOUS OF DOROTHY'S TIME?

JEALOUS?! THANKS FOR THE SUPPORT, MAX. I'LL SOLVE THIS MYSTERY ON MY OWN.

STUART...!

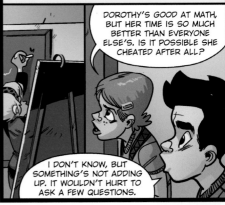

After the rest of the potential presidents tried the maze and got times well over five minutes, we started to change our minds.

DOROTHY'S GOOD AT MATH, BUT HER TIME IS SO MUCH BETTER THAN EVERYONE ELSE'S. IS IT POSSIBLE SHE CHEATED AFTER ALL?

I DON'T KNOW, BUT SOMETHING'S NOT ADDING UP. IT WOULDN'T HURT TO ASK A FEW QUESTIONS.

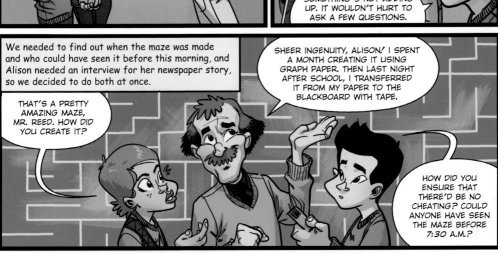

We needed to find out when the maze was made and who could have seen it before this morning, and Alison needed an interview for her newspaper story, so we decided to do both at once.

THAT'S A PRETTY AMAZING MAZE, MR. REED. HOW DID YOU CREATE IT?

SHEER INGENUITY, ALISON! I SPENT A MONTH CREATING IT USING GRAPH PAPER. THEN LAST NIGHT AFTER SCHOOL, I TRANSFERRED IT FROM MY PAPER TO THE BLACKBOARD WITH TAPE.

HOW DID YOU ENSURE THAT THERE'D BE NO CHEATING? COULD ANYONE HAVE SEEN THE MAZE BEFORE 7:30 A.M.?

Not a chance! I finished it at 7:00 p.m. last night, and the only person still here was the school custodian, Mr. P. I was so exhausted by then that I didn't even do a practice run before I locked up and left.

CLICK

I HAVE TO PREPARE FOR CLASS NOW, BUT IF YOU NEED MORE INFO, I TOLD THE OTHER REPORTER EVERYTHING.

WHAT OTHER REPORTER?

THIS OTHER REPORTER! I'VE BEEN HERE ALL MORNING. LOOKS LIKE YOU GOT SCOOPED, SANTOS.

Like Alison, Jake Granger writes stories for our school newspaper, the *Meteor*. He's also my biggest nemesis. This morning, however, he was being a thorn in Alison's side for once.

WHAT ARE YOU DOING HERE, JAKE? THIS IS MY STORY!

WELL, THEN, YOU SHOULD'VE BEEN HERE AT 7:30 A.M. ON THE DOT, LIKE I WAS. YOU KNOW WHAT THEY SAY, SANTOS: EARLY REPORTER GETS THE WORM!

THE ONLY WORM HERE IS...

SO YOU WERE HERE AT 7:30 A.M., YOU SAY?

YEAH, I EVEN GOT A SHOT OF DOROTHY AND MR. REED BEFORE SHE DID THE MAZE. NO OFFENSE TO WHATEVER STORIES YOU'RE WORKING ON THIS WEEK, BUT THAT'S GOING TO BE OUR COVER!

After Jake left for the newspaper office, Alison and I decided to ditch her camera equipment.

BECAUSE JAKE WAS THE ONLY ONE TO GET PHOTOS OF DOROTHY FINISHING THE MAZE, THE NEWSPAPER WILL USE HIS SHOTS INSTEAD OF MINE. IS IT POSSIBLE HE HELPED HER CHEAT SOMEHOW?

OH THERE YOU ARE, MR. P.

SORRY FOR THE DELAY, MS. MUKARNO. I MISPLACED MY CLASSROOM MASTER KEY, BUT MY DAUGHTER FOUND IT FOR ME.

ATTENTION, STUDENTS! THIS IS YOUR PRINCIPAL. IT IS MY PLEASURE TO ANNOUNCE THAT DOROTHY PAFKO IS THE NEW PRESIDENT OF THE MATH CLUB. CONGRATULATIONS, DOROTHY!

HA! DOROTHY CHEATED, AND I HAVE PROOF.

Layne Jennings was another potential math club president. We caught up to her at lunchtime in the cafeteria.

WE HEARD YOU IN THE HALL, LAYNE. HOW DO YOU KNOW THAT DOROTHY CHEATED? DID SHE TELL YOU SOMETHING?

SHE DIDN'T NEED TO! THE PROOF IS IN THE PUDDING, AS THEY SAY.

HER TIME WAS WAY BETTER THAN EVERYONE ELSE'S, AND YET SHE DIDN'T DO ANY PREP WORK AT ALL. WE WERE SUPPOSED TO PRACTICE AT MY HOUSE LAST NIGHT, BUT SHE DIDN'T EVEN SHOW UP!

SORRY, LAYNE, BUT THAT WON'T EXACTLY HOLD UP IN A COURT OF LAW.

LOOKS LIKE THIS CASE, AND THIS MEATLOAF, HAS GONE COLD. THERE MAY BE NO WAY TO TELL IF DOROTHY CHEATED.

DON'T GIVE UP SO EASILY, MAX. I KNOW THE ANSWER, AND I CAN PROVE IT.

Did Dorothy cheat on the maze to become president of the math club? All the clues are here. Turn the page for the solution.

THE CASE OF THE...
MATH CLUB CONUNDRUM

Did Dorothy cheat?

Yes. She had access to the school after hours, so she practiced the maze on the blackboard and memorized it after Mr. Reed went home.

Clues

• Mr. Reed said Dorothy was the first one to do the maze. He also said that after he finished drawing the maze on the blackboard, he didn't take a practice run before he left. That means the corridors of the maze should have been the same green color as the rest of the blackboard.

• However, when Max and Alison looked at the photo on Jake's camera, they noticed that the corridors of the maze were much chalkier than the rest of it. This means that between the time that Mr. Reed finished it and Dorothy tried it the next morning, someone did the maze and then erased the lines to hide the evidence.

• Mr. Reed didn't notice that the board had been erased because he wasn't wearing his glasses.

• In the cafeteria, when Alison saw the name badge on Mr. P's uniform, which read "G. Pafko,"

she realized that Mr. P is actually Mr. Pafko, Dorothy's dad.

• Mr. P said his daughter found his master classroom key for him. That meant that Dorothy had access to the key, which gave her access to Mr. Reed's classroom.

• When Alison saw Dorothy in the cafeteria, she was yawning. That's because she was up late at school figuring out the maze.

Conclusion

When Alison presented her evidence, Dorothy confessed to cheating in order to win the math club presidency. Stuart was named president of the math club, and Mr. Reed vowed to name all his future presidents the old-fashioned way: by vote!

THE CASE OF THE...

COSTUMED CAPER

THE CASE OF THE...
COSTUMED CAPER

Max Finder, junior-high detective, here. Spring had officially sprung. Everyone at our school was outside at lunchtime enjoying the weather.

I FEEL LIKE I HAVEN'T SEEN THE SUN IN YEARS, MAX!

SAME HERE, ALISON. FEELS LIKE WE HAVEN'T SEEN A MYSTERY IN MONTHS EITHER...

LITTERER! STOP IN THE NAME OF JUSTICE!

IT'S THE HALL MONITOR!

Meet the Hall Monitor, our school's very own superhero. What she lacks in actual superpowers, she makes up for with a superhuman sense of right and wrong.

THIS IS MINE, BUT I DIDN'T LITTER! I DIDN'T EVEN KNOW I DROPPED IT!

TELL IT TO THE TRASH CAN, NANDA KANWAR! AND CONSIDER THIS THE NEXT TIME YOU DISRESPECT THE EARTH!

DID YOU SEE THAT, MAX? IT WAS SO COOL!

I DID, ZOE. BUT IT SEEMS LIKE THE HALL MONITOR IS MAKING MORE ENEMIES THAN FRIENDS. SHE SHAMED KYLE KRESSMAN LIKE THAT JUST LAST WEEK.

YOU HAVE TO ADMIT, THOUGH, MAX. THE SCHOOLYARD AND HALLWAYS HAVE NEVER BEEN CLEANER. SHE MUST BE DOING SOMETHING RIGHT.

By the next morning, the Hall Monitor was officially doing everything wrong. We showed up to school to find our classmate Nicholas Musicco talking to our principal, Mr. Lee.

I SAW IT WITH MY OWN EYES, MR. LEE! THE HALL MONITOR EGGED THE SCHOOL!

Nicholas is one of a group of volunteers in our school's safety watch program. He seemed resentful of all the attention the Hall Monitor has gotten lately.

WHAT'S THIS ABOUT, NICHOLAS? HOW DO YOU EVEN KNOW IT WAS THE HALL MONITOR?

OH, IT WAS THE HALL MONITOR, ALL RIGHT! TALL AND SKINNY. SAME BLUE CAPE AND SHOES, TOO!

BACK UP A SECOND. TELL US WHAT YOU SAW FROM THE BEGINNING.

I got to school so early, I thought I was the only one around. When I walked to the main entrance, the Hall Monitor saw me coming, threw two eggs at the front windows, and took off.

WHISPERING MEADOWS HIGH SCHOOL

HEY! STOP!

Dear Central Meadows,

I'm tired of cleaning up your mess... So I'm going to make my own!

Signed,
The Hall Monitor.

I ALSO FOUND THIS IN THE BUSHES BY THE WINDOWS.

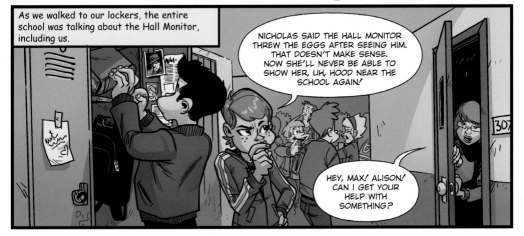

As we walked to our lockers, the entire school was talking about the Hall Monitor, including us.

NICHOLAS SAID THE HALL MONITOR THREW THE EGGS AFTER SEEING HIM. THAT DOESN'T MAKE SENSE. NOW SHE'LL NEVER BE ABLE TO SHOW HER, UH, HOOD NEAR THE SCHOOL AGAIN!

HEY, MAX! ALISON! CAN I GET YOUR HELP WITH SOMETHING?

30?

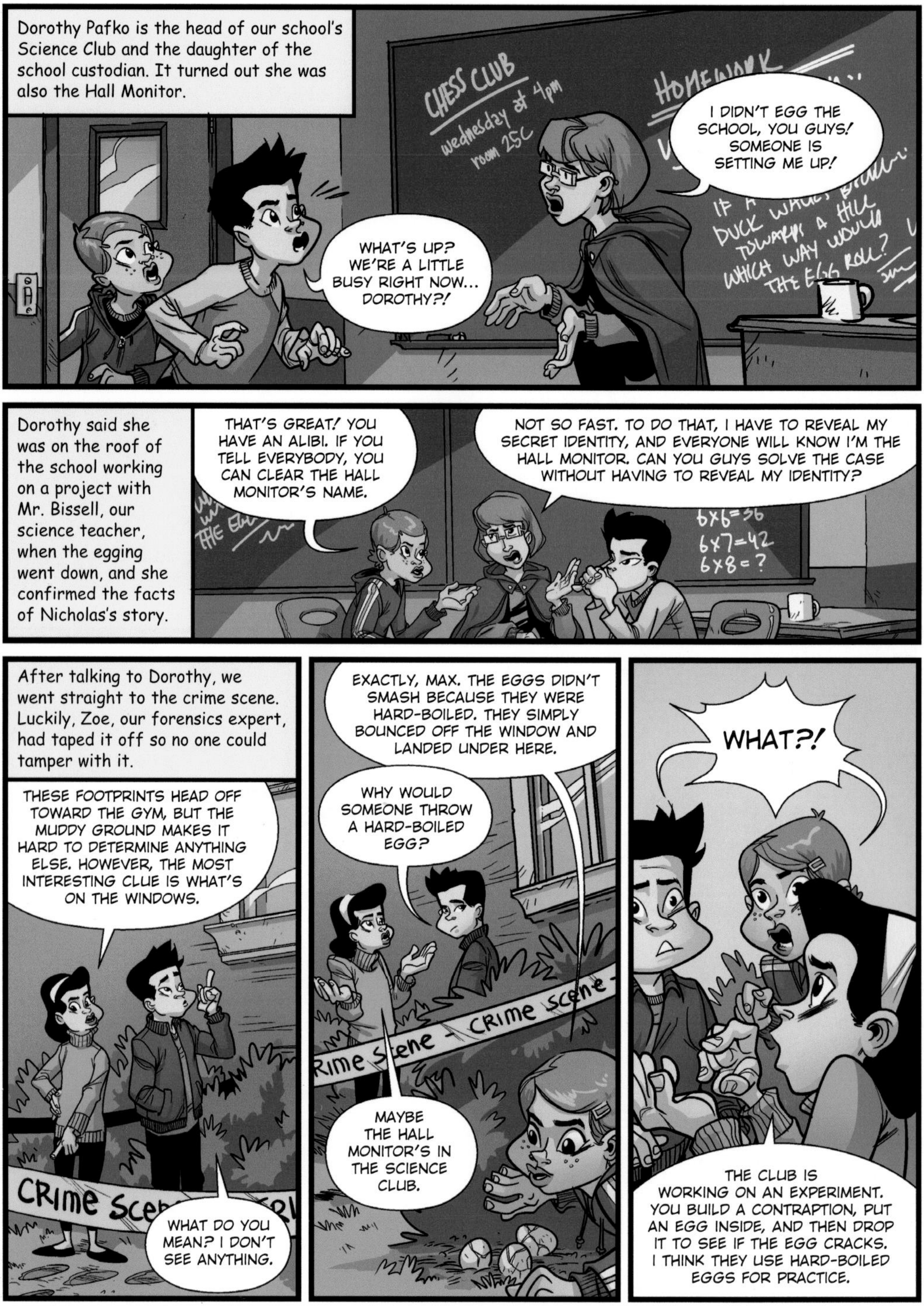

Dorothy Pafko is the head of our school's Science Club and the daughter of the school custodian. It turned out she was also the Hall Monitor.
CHESS CLUB wednesday at 4pm room 25C
WHAT'S UP? WE'RE A LITTLE BUSY RIGHT NOW... DOROTHY?!
I DIDN'T EGG THE SCHOOL, YOU GUYS! SOMEONE IS SETTING ME UP!
Dorothy said she was on the roof of the school working on a project with Mr. Bissell, our science teacher, when the egging went down, and she confirmed the facts of Nicholas's story.
THAT'S GREAT! YOU HAVE AN ALIBI. IF YOU TELL EVERYBODY, YOU CAN CLEAR THE HALL MONITOR'S NAME.
NOT SO FAST. TO DO THAT, I HAVE TO REVEAL MY SECRET IDENTITY, AND EVERYONE WILL KNOW I'M THE HALL MONITOR. CAN YOU GUYS SOLVE THE CASE WITHOUT HAVING TO REVEAL MY IDENTITY?
6x7=42
6x8=?
After talking to Dorothy, we went straight to the crime scene. Luckily, Zoe, our forensics expert, had taped it off so no one could tamper with it.
THESE FOOTPRINTS HEAD OFF TOWARD THE GYM, BUT THE MUDDY GROUND MAKES IT HARD TO DETERMINE ANYTHING ELSE. HOWEVER, THE MOST INTERESTING CLUE IS WHAT'S ON THE WINDOWS.
WHAT DO YOU MEAN? I DON'T SEE ANYTHING.
EXACTLY, MAX. THE EGGS DIDN'T SMASH BECAUSE THEY WERE HARD-BOILED. THEY SIMPLY BOUNCED OFF THE WINDOW AND LANDED UNDER HERE.
WHY WOULD SOMEONE THROW A HARD-BOILED EGG?
CRIME SCENE
MAYBE THE HALL MONITOR'S IN THE SCIENCE CLUB.
WHAT?!
THE CLUB IS WORKING ON AN EXPERIMENT. YOU BUILD A CONTRAPTION, PUT AN EGG INSIDE, AND THEN DROP IT TO SEE IF THE EGG CRACKS. I THINK THEY USE HARD-BOILED EGGS FOR PRACTICE.

The Science Club was meeting outside on the basketball court after school, so Alison and I decided to check it out. Dorothy was nowhere in sight, but we did see Kyle Kressman, our school's biggest prankster.

I'M NOT PART OF THE CLUB, BUT WHAT CAN I SAY? IT'S A GOOD DAY TO WATCH FLYING EGGS, MAX.

YOU DON'T STRIKE ME AS THE SCIENCE CLUB TYPE, KYLE. WHAT'S UP?

SPEAKING OF WHICH, WHERE WERE YOU AROUND THE TIME OF THE EGGING? WORD HAS IT YOU WERE PRETTY MAD AT THE HALL MONITOR FOR BUSTING YOU LAST WEEK.

HOLD YOUR HIGH HORSES, MAX. I FORGOT ABOUT THAT THE MINUTE IT HAPPENED. ALSO, I HAD A DENTIST APPOINTMENT THIS MORNING. I DIDN'T GET HERE UNTIL AFTER FIRST PERIOD.

HEY...WHY ARE YOU BOTHERING KYLE, MAX? EVERYBODY KNOWS THE HALL MONITOR DID IT!

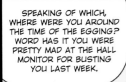

HERE WE GO!

CRACK

WATCH OUT, MAX!

MAX! I'M SO SORRY. I SHOULD'VE LOOKED BEFORE I THREW. ARE YOU ALL RIGHT?

YEAH, I'M ALL RIGHT, THANKS TO KYLE. I'M ALL READY TO CLOSE THIS CASE, TOO. I KNOW WHO EGGED THE SCHOOL THIS MORNING.

Do you know who egged the school? All the clues are here. Turn the page for the solution.

THE CASE OF THE...
COSTUMED CAPER

Who threw the eggs at the school?

Kyle Kressman. He was angry at the Hall Monitor for busting him for littering and tried to frame her to get back at her.

Clues

- Nicholas said that the Hall Monitor was wearing the same blue shoes as always, but the real Hall Monitor wears gray shoes. The only kids wearing blue shoes were Kyle and Nanda.

- Max noticed that Nanda is too small to be described as "tall and skinny." That means only Kyle has the right body type to pass as the Hall Monitor.

- Kyle said he didn't get to school until after first period, but Max and Alison saw him listening to Nicholas's story before school started. He was lying to give himself an alibi.

- Zoe thought the Science Club used hard-boiled eggs for testing their contraptions. She was wrong. Max discovered this when he saw that the egg inside Dorothy's contraption had smashed. That means the eggs didn't come from the Science Club.

- The day that the Hall Monitor caught Nanda for littering, Kyle was in the background peeling a hard-boiled egg. That explains where he got the eggs and why the fake Hall Monitor used hard-boiled eggs in the first place.

Conclusion

When Max presented his evidence, Kyle confessed and pulled the fake Hall Monitor costume from his bag. Because of his recent heroism in helping Max, though, he received only one week of detention instead of two. The real Hall Monitor's secret was safe, but Dorothy decided to retire the hero and do her good deeds without the costume.

THE CASE OF THE...
STOLEN
BASES

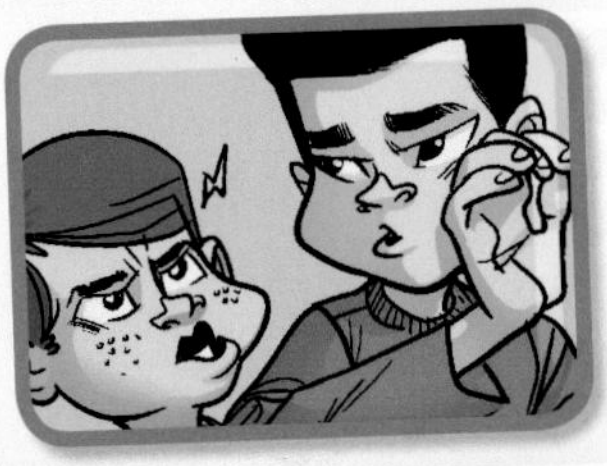

THE CASE OF THE... STOLEN BASES

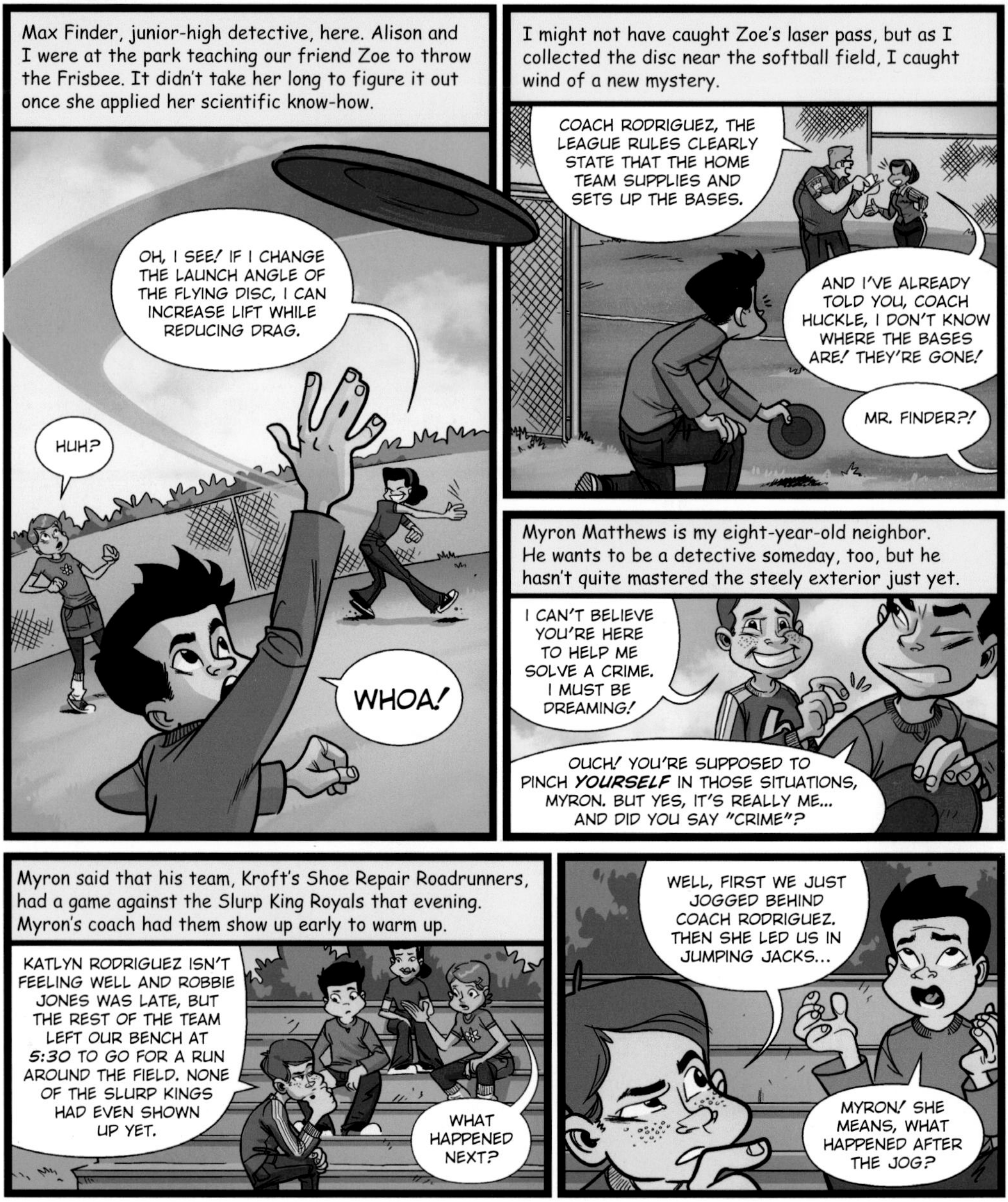

Max Finder, junior-high detective, here. Alison and I were at the park teaching our friend Zoe to throw the Frisbee. It didn't take her long to figure it out once she applied her scientific know-how.
OH, I SEE! IF I CHANGE THE LAUNCH ANGLE OF THE FLYING DISC, I CAN INCREASE LIFT WHILE REDUCING DRAG.
HUH?
WHOA!
I might not have caught Zoe's laser pass, but as I collected the disc near the softball field, I caught wind of a new mystery.
COACH RODRIGUEZ, THE LEAGUE RULES CLEARLY STATE THAT THE HOME TEAM SUPPLIES AND SETS UP THE BASES.
AND I'VE ALREADY TOLD YOU, COACH HUCKLE, I DON'T KNOW WHERE THE BASES ARE! THEY'RE GONE!
MR. FINDER?!
Myron Matthews is my eight-year-old neighbor. He wants to be a detective someday, too, but he hasn't quite mastered the steely exterior just yet.
I CAN'T BELIEVE YOU'RE HERE TO HELP ME SOLVE A CRIME. I MUST BE DREAMING!
OUCH! YOU'RE SUPPOSED TO PINCH ***YOURSELF*** IN THOSE SITUATIONS, MYRON. BUT YES, IT'S REALLY ME... AND DID YOU SAY "CRIME"?
Myron said that his team, Kroft's Shoe Repair Roadrunners, had a game against the Slurp King Royals that evening. Myron's coach had them show up early to warm up.
KATLYN RODRIGUEZ ISN'T FEELING WELL AND ROBBIE JONES WAS LATE, BUT THE REST OF THE TEAM LEFT OUR BENCH AT *5:30* TO GO FOR A RUN AROUND THE FIELD. NONE OF THE SLURP KINGS HAD EVEN SHOWN UP YET.
WHAT HAPPENED NEXT?
WELL, FIRST WE JUST JOGGED BEHIND COACH RODRIGUEZ. THEN SHE LED US IN JUMPING JACKS...
MYRON! SHE MEANS, WHAT HAPPENED AFTER THE JOG?

It took us 15 minutes to run around the park. When we got back, Katlyn and Robbie were sitting on our bench, half the Royals had shown up...and the sports bag with all of our bases in it was gone.

WHAT HAPPENED TO THE BASES?!

WE SUGGESTED PLAYING WITHOUT THE BASES, BUT COACH HUCKLE SAID THAT'S AGAINST THE RULES. IF WE DON'T FIND THEM WITHIN 30 MINUTES OF GAME TIME, WE AUTOMATICALLY LOSE.

AND THE GAME'S SUPPOSED TO START RIGHT NOW.

Lucky for Myron and the rest of the Roadrunners, Zoe is the best amateur forensic expert in Whispering Meadows. In just a couple of minutes she was onto the base bandit's trail...literally.

THE WIDTH OF THIS TRAIL MATCHES MYRON'S DESCRIPTION OF THE SPORTS BAG. SEEMS LIKE SOMEONE DRAGGED THE BASES TOWARD RIGHT FIELD.

GOOD FIND, ZOE, BUT THE TRAIL GOES COLD WHEN IT HITS THE SHORT GRASS IN THE OUTFIELD. LOOKS LIKE WE'D BETTER FOCUS ON FINDING SOME WITNESSES.

I KNOW JUST WHERE TO START.

THEN THAT DOESN'T GIVE US A LOT OF TIME! LET ME AT THAT CRIME SCENE.

Myron told us that Katlyn Rodriguez doesn't like softball, but she can't quit the team because her mom is the coach. She was still nursing her stomachache when we caught up with her.

I WAS HERE THE WHOLE TIME, BUT I WAS TOO BUSY HOLDING MY TUMMY! I DIDN'T SEE ANYTHING!

IT SEEMS LIKE THE BASES WERE STOLEN RIGHT AFTER YOUR MOM LEFT TO TAKE THE TEAM FOR A JOG AROUND THE FIELD. DID YOU SEE WHO DID IT?

WELL, DID YOU HEAR ANYTHING? SOMEONE DRAGGING OFF A SPORTS BAG FULL OF BASES WOULD MAKE A LOT OF NOISE.

YOU SHOULD TALK TO ROBBIE JONES. HE WAS HERE, TOO, AND HE LOOKS REALLY NERVOUS ABOUT SOMETHING. MAYBE HE TOOK THE BASES!

SEEMS LIKE KATLYN IS HIDING SOMETHING. MAYBE SHE TOOK THE BASES TO GET A NIGHT OFF FROM PLAYING.

IT'S POSSIBLE, MYRON, BUT WE NEED MORE FACTS. WE'D BETTER TALK TO ROBBIE.

Myron helped us track down Robbie in his "happy place"—the park snack bar near the soccer fields. Katlyn was right about at least one thing: the skinny pitching sensation looked nervous.

IF YOU DON'T MIND ME SAYING SO, ROBBIE, YOU LOOK A LITTLE SCARED ABOUT SOMETHING...

SHH! THE LAST TIME WE PLAYED THE ROYALS, THEY HIT FIVE HOME RUNS OFF ME. I'M SCARED TO PITCH TO THEM TONIGHT, BUT I DON'T WANT THEM TO KNOW THAT!

THEY'RE ALSO THE MEANEST TEAM IN TOWN, AND THEY'RE ONLY GETTING MEANER. SMASHER MCGINTLEY IS ON THEIR TEAM NOW, TOO.

SORRY... DID YOU SAY "SMASHER"?

Ben "Basher" McGintley is the biggest bully at Central Meadows Junior High. As I found out, his cousin Sarah is only nine years old, but she's every bit as much of a bully.

MR. FINDER, MEET SMASHER. WHEN WE LEFT FOR OUR JOG, SHE SHOWED UP AND THE BASES WENT MISSING. SEEMS LIKE A PRETTY BIG *CONFIDENCE* TO ME.

THAT'S "COINCIDENCE," MYRON.

WHATEVER, TWERP! WHEN MY TEAM GOT HERE, ROBBIE JONES WAS ALL ALONE IN THE ROADRUNNER DUGOUT, AND THE BASES WERE ALREADY GONE.

DO YOU HAPPEN TO KNOW WHERE THE BASES MIGHT BE?

MY COUSIN TOLD ME ABOUT YOU, MAX FINDER. LOOK, I DIDN'T TOUCH THE BASES, AND I DON'T KNOW WHO DID. NOW BUZZ OFF!

Our 30 minutes were almost up, and so was the coaches' patience.

WE ALL KNOW YOU TOOK THE BASES, COACH!

HOW DO WE KNOW YOU DIDN'T HIDE THE BASES YOURSELF TO AVOID HUMILIATION?

TIME OUT!

YOU TWO CAN SETTLE THIS ARGUMENT ON THE FIELD. I KNOW WHO TOOK THE BASES.

AND I KNOW WHERE THEY ARE.

Do you know who stole the bases? All the clues are here. Turn the page for the solution.

61

THE CASE OF THE...
STOLEN BASES

Who stole the Roadrunners' bases?

Robbie Jones. He was afraid to pitch against the Royals, so he buried the bases to get the game canceled.

Clues

• When Max, Alison, and Zoe walked by the construction area behind the restrooms, Alison noticed the sign said "Danger! Open Hole," but the hole was closed in. That's how she knew where the bases were.

• Max noticed Robbie had dirty hands and dirt under his fingernails, while Smasher and Katlyn both had clean hands.

• While the coaches were arguing, the players on both teams were in uniform and ready to play—except Robbie. He had his jacket on. He was expecting the game to be canceled because he had stolen the bases.

• When Smasher and her teammates showed up to the field, only Robbie Jones was sitting in the Roadrunners' dugout. That explains why Katlyn didn't see or hear anything.

• Katlyn said she had a stomachache, but Max and Alison noticed she was eating licorice as the coaches argued. It was the same kind for sale at the snack bar.

• Myron said that his team's jog around the field took 15 minutes. That gave Katlyn lots of time to get to the snack bar and back—and Robbie lots of time to drag off the bases and bury them by the restrooms.

• The detectives saw Smasher lift up her team's equipment bag with ease. That means she wouldn't have needed to drag the Roadrunners' bag and leave a trail.

Conclusion

When Max and Alison presented their evidence, Robbie confessed to the crime. Coach Rodriguez benched him for a month and put Myron in as his last-minute pitching replacement against the Royals. Both teams played well, and the Roadrunners squeaked out a 5–4 victory.

The Case of the
Ice Cream Parlor
Pickpocket

As told by Max Finder

FROM: Max Finder <sooprsleuth@hypemail.com>
DATE: July 15 at 10:12 AM
SUBJECT: Hello, Port Charlotte!
TO: Alison Santos <dtektvgrrl@yeehaw.ca>

Dear Alison,
I'm writing this on my cell phone. I figured this would be easier—and quicker—than sending postcards.

My mom and I just pulled up at my aunt and uncle's house in Port Charlotte, BC. It's BEAUTIFUL here! So many trees. We even saw a family of deer as we drove in from the airport. My aunt and uncle live so close to the ocean you can hear it from their front yard—that is, if you could hear anything over my 13-year-old cousin, Lena. As soon as I got out of the car, she practically tackled me with a hug, saying she couldn't wait to introduce me to her friends.

Lena's taking me downtown now. Everything's located pretty much on one street—post office, fire station, corner store, antique shop, and so on. She said something about hitting up the ice cream parlor. Guess you could say the vacation's off to a great start!

Yours in detection,
Max Finder

FROM: Max Finder <sooprsleuth@hypemail.com>
DATE: July 15 at 10:49 AM
SUBJECT: Hello, Port Trouble!
TO: Alison Santos <dtektvgrrl@yeehaw.ca>

Dear Alison,
Hey, can you send me my mystery radar? I think I left it at home. Two seconds after I'd waved good-bye to my mom, Lena grabbed me by both arms and filled me in on the real nature of our trip downtown.

"Max, you've got to help me!" she said. "Something's been stolen!"

It turns out Lena recently found a mint-condition first issue of her favorite comic series—Captain Adventure—in the local antique shop. Her parents offered to help her pay for it, with one catch. She had to promise to keep it safe.

"It took one afternoon for me to mess that up," Lena said. "But it wasn't my fault. Someone took it from me. And I need you to help me get it back."

We hurried downtown and set up behind some trash cans in the alley across the street from Sprinkles Ice Cream Parlor. The parlor was big and pretty packed. There was a counter with a couple of employees behind it, a long metal bar with stools all along the front window, and several small tables. There were even a couple of old pinball machines on the far side: Wizard's Quest and Bumper Baseball.

"When I got to the parlor, I was carrying the comic in my backpack. I showed it to my friend Cindy at the bar up front. She was happy for me but didn't seem too impressed with the comic itself. Then I pushed napkins and ice cream spoons out of the way and put the backpack down on the bar."

"What time was this?" I asked.

"Just after 1:00," Lena said. "I asked Cindy to watch the backpack while I went to the counter for a double scoop of rocky road. When I got back, Cindy was on the other side of the parlor playing pinball in front of a crowd of kids. The backpack was there, but the comic wasn't. I thought it might have fallen out, but it was nowhere in sight—the area around my backpack was wiped clean and spotless!"

My suspect list was starting to take shape. Lena added that two other people in the parlor at the time might have had a motive to steal the comic from her: Tyson Tarr, an employee at the parlor and huge comic fan, and Mr. Smith, the owner of the antique shop where she bought it.

"He just sold you the comic," I said. "Why would he want to steal it back?"

"Well, uh, that's the thing," she stammered. "I kind of stole it from him."

"What?!" I shouted, standing up.

Lena grabbed me and dragged me back down so I wouldn't draw attention. "It's not like that," she said. "I just got a really good deal. It's super-rare and worth hundreds, but Mr. Smith charged me only $50 for it. He might have found out afterward what it was worth and been mad about selling it to me so cheap."

So that's where we're at, Alison. Please find me my mystery radar. I'm going to go find Cindy.

More soon,
Max

FROM: Max Finder <sooprsleuth@hypemail.com>
DATE: July 15 at 11:52 AM
SUBJECT: Cindy
TO: Alison Santos <dtektvgrrl@yeehaw.ca>

Hey…again,
Where were we? Oh yeah. Cindy. Just for the record, her name's Cindy Schaeffer. She's 13 as well. She's tall with blond hair and green eyes. I left Lena in the alley and found Cindy in the ice cream parlor playing pinball on the same machine Lena told me about: Wizard's Quest. It glows orange and has a picture of a white-haired wizard staring out at players, and every time the steel ball passes through a certain spot, a deep voice says, "Magic!"

"Can I talk to you for a second?" I asked, sidling up beside the game as she smacked the plunger and sent a ball flying up into the machine.

"I don't know," she said, chuckling. "Can you?"

I introduced myself and told her I was looking for the comic.

"Oh, Lena's Adventure Town comic? What, did she lose it somewhere?"

"No, it was stolen," I said. "While you were supposed to be looking after it." At this, Cindy's face dropped. So did her ball, ending her game. She smacked the paddles in frustration.

"Do you mind telling me what you saw while Lena was getting ice cream?" I asked.

"She said she'd be gone a minute, but it was more like ten," Cindy said. "The line for ice cream was so long, and I got bored of waiting for her to come back. I planned to be gone for only a minute or two to play a quick game of pinball, but then I had the game of my life. I couldn't just leave it! I even ended up with the all-time high score."

While we were talking, the manager of the parlor came by with an ice cream server to take a look at the Wizard's Quest machine, and Cindy left to find Lena and apologize. As I was standing there, I overheard a snippet of the technical conversation. "It's strange," the manager said. "A rectangular area in the bottom right corner of the vertical board isn't lighting up, but a technician just changed those bulbs last week. It was fine all day yesterday. I noticed it right before we closed up."

They left unable to figure out the issue but convinced it wasn't a problem with the bulbs. Anyway: one mystery at a time. I checked the high scores and found no "CS" or anything like that at the top of the leaderboard. The number-one name on the list was "LOL."

Off to ponder,
Max

FROM: Max Finder <sooprsleuth@hypemail.com>
DATE: July 15 at 12:45 PM
SUBJECT: Tyson
TO: Alison Santos <dtektvgrrl@yeehaw.ca>

Hey Al,
Thanks for the email. I took your advice and talked to Tyson Tarr before I left the ice cream parlor. He was wearing a white smock and paper hat like all the other employees in the shop. Unlike the other employees, though, he was the only one who tidied up after messy customers. "I hear you're a big comic fan," I said to him after I'd ordered a small soda.

"Guilty as charged, Mr. Detective," he said, causing me to do a double take. "Lena tells us about you all the time. You're famous around here."

Tyson told me he isn't just a big comic fan—he's the BIGGEST comic fan. He collects everything from Kid Cheetah to Dr. Mindfantastic. He has a poster on his wall depicting the long-awaited face-off between the X-cellents and the No-Nonsense Nine. But, he said, he had no idea there was even a copy of *Captain Adventure #1* anywhere in Port Charlotte.

"So Lena bought it from the antique store and had it stolen from here?" he asked.

"Yeah, just about 1:00 yesterday," I told him. "You would have been working then, right? Maybe you saw something suspicious when you were doing your cleanup rounds?"

"I might have if I'd had any time for them," Tyson said. "Yesterday was one of the busiest days we've ever had. I was helping out behind the counter for most of the afternoon and didn't get to do a cleanup until well after 2:00. I had to skip my break and didn't stop moving 'til we locked up."

I went outside and found Lena in the alley. She confirmed that Tyson was in the parlor until closing time.

"I hung around all the rest of the day, hoping to see someone walk off with the comic. Tyson left at 6:00 with the manager. He was wearing shorts and a T-shirt, and he wasn't carrying anything."

"Maybe he had the comic tucked under his shirt?" I offered, but Lena quickly shut me down.

"Not a chance," she said. "That would risk bending and ripping it, which would ruin its resale value. No way he'd do that to a comic."

Speaking of resale value, can you check to see if any copies of *Captain Adventure #1* have hit the auction sites? Lena tells me Cindy is a big fan of eBuy…

Max

FROM: Max Finder <sooprsleuth@hypemail.com>
DATE: July 15 at 1:28 PM
SUBJECT: Mr. Smith
TO: Alison Santos <dtektvgrrl@yeehaw.ca>

Hey,

Nothing on the auction sites, huh? It figures. Our criminal is too smart for that. Anyway, it was nearing 1:00 when I stepped out of the alley to go talk to Mr. Smith. It was about the same time when Mr. Smith knocked me flat, walking in a hurry back to his shop.

"I'm so sorry, young man!" he said, helping me up off the sidewalk. "I didn't see you there."

Mr. Smith is a precise-looking older man with sharply parted silver hair. His eyes always seem to be appraising things. We made introductions, and I told him I was Lena's cousin. At that, his smile disappeared. I took the opportunity to ask innocently about the comic.

"I heard Lena bought something from your shop the other day. A comic book or something?"

"It was a first edition of the first issue of Captain Adventure!" he told me excitedly. "I had no idea what it was actually worth until young Mr. Tarr told me about it."

"Oh, really?" I said, feigning surprise. "Sounds expensive!"

"It *should* have been," he said, reddening. "I didn't find out what it was worth until after I sold it. I specialize in old and rare furniture and stumbled upon the comic in a box of old stuff I bought at an estate sale. How am I supposed to know what it's worth?"

Mr. Smith was checking his watch. I decided to shift gears. "You were at the ice cream parlor yesterday afternoon, right?"

"Yes," Mr. Smith said, suddenly confused. "Why?"

"The comic was stolen from there right around the time you were there. Lena says you ducked out rather quickly, but I was hoping you might have seen something suspicious."

"I…I close the antique shop between 12:30 and 1:00. I had to be back to open it up." He looked at his watch one more time. "Egad! I have to run."

Lena emerged from the alley, and we tailed him down to the store. He unlocked the front door, leaped inside, and flipped the "Closed" sign to "Open." I checked my watch. It was exactly 1:00.

"He does that every day," Lena said, pointing at the hours in the window. "He sticks to those like clockwork. He closes up at exactly 12:30 and reopens at exactly 1:00."

In the shop window I noticed a few posters for different events around town. One poster was for a stand-up comedy show and featured a picture of a certain tall girl I know. "You'll laugh out loud!" it read.

That's when I told Lena she could buy me an ice cream to thank me. "Thank you for what?" she asked.

"For catching a thief. I know who stole the comic. I know where it is, too."

Do you know who stole the comic?
Turn the page for the solution.

THE CASE OF THE...
ICE CREAM PARLOR PICKPOCKET

Who stole the Captain Adventure comic?

Tyson Tarr. He was jealous that Lena got to the comic before him, and he stole it so he could have it for himself.

Clues

- Lena said she had to push napkins and sundae spoons out of the way to put her backpack down the day the comic was stolen, but that the area was spotless when she was looking for her comic. That means someone came through to clean up. The only employee at the shop who does that is Tyson.

- Tyson said he didn't even know that Lena had bought the comic, but Mr. Smith said that he did.

- When Max was listening in on the conversation about the pinball machine, he learned that an area at the bottom of the machine wasn't lighting up—even though the bulbs were working. That meant something was blocking the lights from shining out. It was the comic. Since the problem showed up after the day was over, that means only Tyson could have hidden it there.

- Cindy didn't even know the name of the comic (she called it Adventure Town, not Captain Adventure), so it's unlikely she'd know what it was worth.

- The poster in Mr. Smith's window told Max that Cindy was an aspiring stand-up comic. That's why the initials at the top of the Wizard's Quest leaderboard said "LOL." She was telling the truth when she said she got the high score. That also explains why so many kids were crowding around the pinball machine when the comic was stolen.

- Lena told Max the comic was stolen just after 1:00. She also said that Mr. Smith sticks to his hours like clockwork. That means he couldn't have stolen the comic. He only closes between 12:30 and 1:00.

Conclusion

When Max presented his evidence, Tyson confessed. He pulled the comic out of a small panel in the front of the pinball machine and returned it to Lena. Max emailed Alison one more time to thank her for her help, and she replied with only four words: "NOW ENJOY YOUR VACATION!"

THE CASE OF THE...
MISSING MASCOT

THE CASE OF THE...
MISSING MASCOT

Max Finder, junior-high detective, here. It was the day of our school's annual photo, and Zoe, Alison, and I were headed outside with all of our classmates.

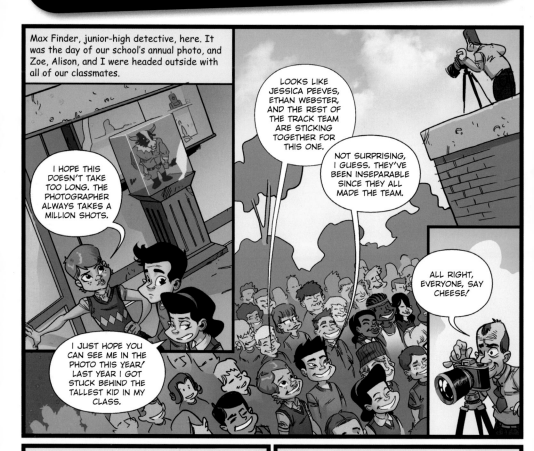

LOOKS LIKE JESSICA PEEVES, ETHAN WEBSTER, AND THE REST OF THE TRACK TEAM ARE STICKING TOGETHER FOR THIS ONE.

NOT SURPRISING, I GUESS. THEY'VE BEEN INSEPARABLE SINCE THEY ALL MADE THE TEAM.

I HOPE THIS DOESN'T TAKE TOO LONG. THE PHOTOGRAPHER ALWAYS TAKES A MILLION SHOTS.

ALL RIGHT, EVERYONE, SAY CHEESE!

I JUST HOPE YOU CAN SEE ME IN THE PHOTO THIS YEAR! LAST YEAR I GOT STUCK BEHIND THE TALLEST KID IN MY CLASS.

Once the shots were taken, we all headed back inside. We'd been gone only 20 minutes, but someone had managed to commit the crime of the century.

SOMEONE'S STOLEN MANNY!

Manny the Minotaur is a stuffed animal. He's also our school's mascot. Mr. Lee, our principal, believed he had just been misplaced.

BUT, MR. LEE, WE CAN'T RACE WITHOUT MANNY. HE'S OUR GOOD LUCK CHARM!

DON'T WORRY, JESSICA. I'LL MAKE AN ANNOUNCEMENT. I'M SURE HE'LL SHOW UP BEFORE THE TRACK MEET.

It was clear the track team didn't think Mr. Lee was taking the situation seriously enough. I didn't either. Manny is taken out of his case only on event days, and then only by Mr. Lee himself.

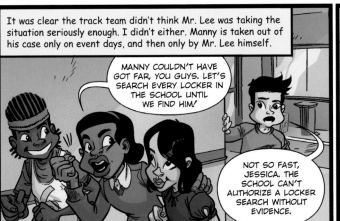

MANNY COULDN'T HAVE GOT FAR, YOU GUYS. LET'S SEARCH EVERY LOCKER IN THE SCHOOL UNTIL WE FIND HIM!

NOT SO FAST, JESSICA. THE SCHOOL CAN'T AUTHORIZE A LOCKER SEARCH WITHOUT EVIDENCE.

THEN YOU'D BETTER GET ON IT, MAX! THE TRACK MEET DEPENDS ON IT.

With that vote of confidence, we turned to the crime scene. Zoe quickly started retracing the thief's steps. Maybe a little too quickly.

THE GLASS CASE IS HEAVY. THE THIEF WOULD'VE NEEDED BOTH HANDS TO SET IT DOWN, LIKE THIS. THEN...

ZOE...!

OUCH!

WHUMP

WELL, THAT WAS A WASTE OF TIME... AND A HAIR BAND.

I WOULDN'T SAY THAT, ZOE. I'VE GOT BOTH YOUR HAIR BAND AND A CLUE.

Courtney LeGuin is a member of the school's Green Thumb Club and loves tropical flowers—especially in her hair. We tracked her down at the end of the day.

HI, COURTNEY. I THINK THIS BELONGS TO YOU.

OH, THANK YOU, MAX! I THOUGHT IT WAS GONE FOREVER. WHERE DID YOU FIND IT?

THE SCENE OF THIS MORNING'S MASCOT HEIST. CAN YOU TELL US WHERE YOU WERE WHEN A CERTAIN MASCOT WAS STOLEN?

WHAT ARE YOU TRYING TO SAY, MAX? I WAS OUTSIDE GETTING MY PICTURE TAKEN LIKE EVERYBODY ELSE.

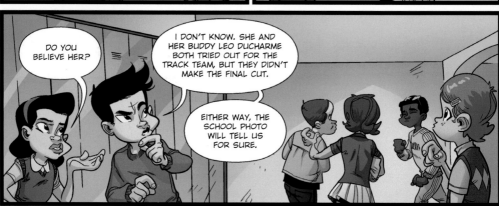

DO YOU BELIEVE HER?

I DON'T KNOW. SHE AND HER BUDDY LEO DUCHARME BOTH TRIED OUT FOR THE TRACK TEAM, BUT THEY DIDN'T MAKE THE FINAL CUT.

EITHER WAY, THE SCHOOL PHOTO WILL TELL US FOR SURE.

THEN IT LOOKS LIKE WE'RE STUCK. I HEARD THAT THE PHOTOGRAPHER ISN'T DROPPING OFF THE DIGITAL PRINTS UNTIL TOMORROW.

MAYBE SO, ZOE, BUT THAT DOESN'T MEAN WE CAN'T CHASE DOWN SOME OTHER LEADS IN THE MEANTIME.

WHAT LEADS?

THE FACT THAT JAKE IS WEARING THE TRACK SUIT OF THE TWINDALE TORNADOES, OUR BIGGEST RIVALS IN THE UPCOMING TRACK MEET.

Jake Granger is an amateur magician and detective...not to mention my nemesis.

WHAT'S THE DEAL, JAKE? WEARING THAT SUIT DURING TRACK SEASON MAKES IT SEEM LIKE YOU'RE WORKING FOR THE OTHER TEAM.

VERY FUNNY, SANTOS! LIKE I HAVEN'T HAD A HARD ENOUGH WEEK ALREADY.

YOU'RE HOLDING UP THE LINE, JAKE!

The next morning, Alison and I showed up early at the school's office to check up on Courtney's alibi. It turned out she was telling the truth after all.

WE NOTICED YOU WEREN'T IN THE SCHOOL PHOTO, LEO. WHY NOT?

I AM TOO! YOU JUST CAN'T SEE ME.

THERE SHE IS. STANDING OFF TO THE SIDE OF THE BACK ROW.

THAT'S TRUE, MAX, BUT I'M MORE INTERESTED IN WHO'S ABSENT.

THAT EXCUSE WOULDN'T HOLD UP IN A COURT OF LAW, LEO. WHERE WERE YOU STANDING?

I WAS IN THE BACK, I SWEAR. I GOTTA GO, MAX.

SLAM

HOW'S YOUR WEEK OF TORMENT GOING, JAKE?

WELL, GUYS, I HAVE MY HUNCHES, BUT I'M STUMPED FOR EVIDENCE.

DON'T WORRY, MAX. I KNOW WHO MINOTAUR-NAPPED MANNY. AND I CAN PROVE IT.

I LOST A BET TO KYLE KRESSMAN AND ALL I GOT WAS THIS T-SHIRT

Do you know who stole Manny the Minotaur? All the clues are here. Turn the page for the solution.

THE CASE OF THE...
MISSING MASCOT

Who stole Manny the Minotaur?

Courtney LeGuin (with help from her friend Leo Ducharme). They were mad about not making the team, so they stole Manny to get revenge.

Clues

- When Max and Alison saw the school photo, Courtney LeGuin was in it. But upon further study, Alison noticed that Courtney was standing off to the side and wearing the same clothes that Leo was wearing on the day the photo was taken. It wasn't Courtney at all. It was Leo.

- Alison noticed that Leo had a curly brown wig and a mask made of a picture of Courtney's face on the floor of his locker.

- When Max and Alison approached Courtney at her locker, she was holding an ice pack under her arm. That's because she bumped her head when she put down the mascot's glass case, and that's why her hair clip fell in the same spot as Zoe's hair band after she hit her head.

- Jake Granger may have been wearing a Twindale track suit, but he didn't steal the mascot. Max and Alison noticed him in the school photo, near where Leo was standing. He was wearing the track suit because he lost a bet with the school's biggest prankster, Kyle Kressman.

Conclusion

After Alison gave her evidence, Courtney confessed and said it was all her idea. She said they were angry because they wanted to be part of the team. When she returned Manny (he was hidden in her locker), Mr. Lee sentenced her and Leo to two months of community service—as equipment managers for the track team.

THE CASE OF THE...
RUINED RELAY

THE CASE OF THE...
RUINED RELAY

Max Finder, junior-high detective, here. When Alison was added to the Central Meadows relay team for the district track meet, I had to go and support her. Andrea, sister of our friend Zoe, was running the first leg for the team.

I'M SO NERVOUS, MAX!

DON'T WORRY, ZOE. WE'RE THE BEST SQUAD ON THE TRACK. ONLY TWINDALE STANDS A CHANCE AGAINST US.

OKAY, I'VE GOT IT, ANDREA. LET GO!

I'M TRYING, ALISON!

Andrea and Alison completed the pass, but the team lost several valuable seconds and finished a distant fourth. By the time we got to the finish line, Jessica Peeves, team captain and relay anchor, was fuming.

I DON'T KNOW WHAT HAPPENED, BUT SOMETHING WASN'T RIGHT WITH OUR BATON!

IT'S TRUE, MAX. I JUST COULDN'T PRY IT OUT OF ANDREA'S HANDS. I THINK SOMEONE TAMPERED WITH OUR BATON TO RUIN OUR CHANCES OF WINNING.

Alison left for her next event, so we inspected the evidence. It wasn't surprising that Zoe had brought her forensics kit with her. It was surprising, however, what she discovered with it.

HMM, INTERESTING. THIS BATON IS COATED WITH A SURPLUS AMOUNT OF ADHESIVE PASTE.

SORRY, ZOE? IN ENGLISH?

STICKY STUFF, MAX! ATHLETES USE IT TO GET A GOOD GRIP IN SPORTS LIKE WEIGHTLIFTING AND POLE VAULTING. BUT IT'S A BAD FIT FOR A RELAY RACE, ESPECIALLY WHEN SO MUCH OF IT IS USED AT ONCE.

ALISON WAS RIGHT. IT'S SABOTAGE.

Now that we'd figured out the nature of the crime, Zoe and I set about gathering witnesses. We started with Andrea.

JESSICA'S SO MAD! BUT I SWEAR IT WASN'T MY FAULT.

WE KNOW, ANDREA. WE THINK SOMEONE TAMPERED WITH YOUR BATON BEFORE THE RACE. CAN YOU TELL US WHERE YOU GOT IT?

I took a short walk to calm my nerves before the race. By the time I grabbed our baton from race organizer John Chu at the scorer's table, it was the last one there.

MY HANDS WERE SO SWEATY I DIDN'T NOTICE ANYTHING WAS WRONG WITH THE BATON.

LET'S GO, ANDREA! YOU'RE UP NEXT!

Our next step was to track down John Chu. He goes to Whispering Meadows High School, and he was volunteering at the track meet for class credit.

I INSPECTED THE BATONS AND LABELED THEM WITH A BLACK MARKER. THREE OF THE GIRLS IN THE RACE PICKED UP THEIR BATONS AT THE SAME TIME, AND THEY WERE ALL FINE.

GO ASK ANA GUZMAN. SHE WAS HERE JUST AS I FINISHED LABELING THEM!

Ana Guzman was also on the Central Meadows relay team. She comes from a sporty family, and her dad was even a famous Olympic pole vaulter. We tracked her down at the long jump pit.

I'D MOVE OVER IF I WERE YOU, MAX.

WHY...?

THAT'S WHY!

As I brushed off an entire beach's worth of sand, Ana took off for her next event. Luckily, Jessica Peeves did our questioning for us.

DID YOU HEAR, ANA? THERE'S A RUMOR GOING AROUND THAT SOMEONE TAMPERED WITH OUR BATON. I THOUGHT YOU SAID YOU CHECKED IT BEFORE THE RACE!

I DID. THEY WERE ALL FINE WHEN I WAS HANGING OUT WITH JOHN AT THE SCORER'S TABLE. BUT I NOTICED SOMETHING ELSE...

AS I WAS LEAVING THE TABLE, I SAW SHAWNA CARVER WALKING OVER THERE. SHE COULD'VE TAMPERED WITH THE CENTRAL MEADOWS BATON WHEN I WASN'T LOOKING!

Shawna Carver is a member of Twindale's relay team. We've tracked her down while working on cases in the past, both as a source and as a suspect.

WE THINK SOMEONE SABOTAGED THE CENTRAL MEADOWS BATON BEFORE THE RELAY RACE. YOU WOULDN'T HAPPEN TO KNOW ANYTHING ABOUT THAT, WOULD YOU?

WE WON FAIR AND SQUARE, MAX. I PICKED UP MY BATON FROM THE TABLE WITH TWO OTHER GIRLS, AND THAT'S IT.

SPEAKING OF BATONS, WILL YOU TAKE THIS BACK TO JOHN FOR ME? HE WAS BUSY ON HIS TABLET AND JUST TOLD US TO PICK OUR OWN BATONS. I MUST'VE GRABBED THE CENTRAL MEADOWS ONE BY MISTAKE.

We met up with Alison as she was finishing her day's events. She had won us a medal in the triple jump, but she looked quadruple depressed.

DON'T WORRY, ALISON. THIS SITUATION WON'T BE STICKY FOR MUCH LONGER. I KNOW WHAT HAPPENED TO THE BATON.

I JUST TALKED TO JESSICA, GUYS. SHE THINKS TWINDALE SABOTAGED US IN THE RELAY. SHE'S GOING TO TELL THE OFFICIALS RIGHT NOW.

AND I KNOW WHO DID IT.

Do you know who sabotaged the Central Meadows relay team? All the clues are here. Turn the page for the solution.

THE CASE OF THE...
RUINED RELAY

Who sabotaged the Central Meadows relay team?

Ana Guzman. She wanted to give Central Meadows an edge by sabotaging the Twindale baton, but her plan backfired when Shawna Carver picked up the Central Meadows baton by accident.

Clues

• When Zoe was examining the sticky baton, she noticed it said "TW" on it. It wasn't until Shawna mentioned picking up the Central Meadows baton by mistake that she realized the "TW" was the beginning of "Twindale." (The rest of the word had rubbed off because John wrote it with a dry-erase marker.) That means whoever sabotaged the baton thought they were sabotaging Twindale, not Central Meadows.

• John said Ana showed up at the scorer's table just after he finished labeling the batons. That gave her the opportunity to sabotage the Twindale baton.

• Ana's father was a world-class pole vaulter. That means he would have adhesive paste to help him grip his equipment, which explains where Ana would get it.

• As Ana was talking to Jessica near the long jump pit, Max noticed a small jar sticking out of her bag. It said "Stick to It! Adhesive Paste for Athletes." That's what Ana used to sabotage the baton.

• When Max and Zoe were talking to John, they noticed he was busy looking at a tablet computer. It was marked "Property of A. Guzman." Ana gave it to him to distract him while she sabotaged the Twindale baton.

Conclusion

When Max and Zoe presented their evidence to race officials, they cleared the Twindale team of the crime and upheld their victory in the relay. Ana apologized for trying to sabotage her rivals and vowed never to cheat again—when her coaches let her back on the team, that is!

THE CASE OF THE...

PUZZLING PUPPET MASTER

THE CASE OF THE...
PUZZLING PUPPET MASTER

Max Finder, junior-high detective, here. It was a sunny summer morning and I was just finishing breakfast. That is, until my best friend, Alison, busted down my front door.

SLAM

MAX! YOU'VE GOT TO SEE SOMETHING. NOW!

I WAS READING TODAY'S PAPER AND SAW THIS. I THOUGHT IT WAS A GAME, BUT IT'S NOT. IT'S A CODED MESSAGE.

MI OGGIN OT EALST HETTNAIHNM YUMMM RGFM ETH SJUEMMTA :002 MP OAYDI HTCAC EM FIYUO CNA, AXM FRINDEI DENGIS, - YMOTARYIR

DID YOU FIGURE IT OUT?

IT SAYS, "I'M GOING TO STEAL THE THINMAN MUMMY FROM THE MUSEUM AT 2:00 P.M. TODAY! CATCH ME IF YOU CAN, MAX FINDER! SIGNED, MORIARTY"!

The Thinman Mummy is our museum's most famous exhibit, and Moriarty is the nemesis of my favorite detective, Sherlock Holmes. Whoever sent that note knew a lot about me.

I quickly changed, and we hit the newspaper office to track down the identity of our "Moriarty." We found Fran Freeman. She used to work at my mom's TV station. She told us she never saw who placed the ad.

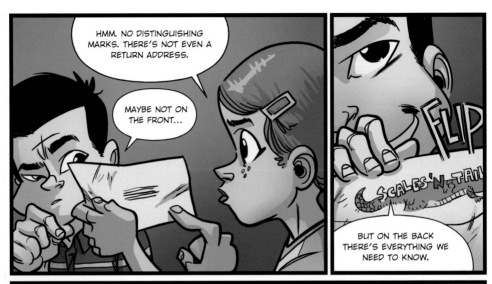

HMM. NO DISTINGUISHING MARKS. THERE'S NOT EVEN A RETURN ADDRESS.

MAYBE NOT ON THE FRONT...

BUT ON THE BACK THERE'S EVERYTHING WE NEED TO KNOW.

I didn't know if we could trust Fran. When she lost her job at the TV station, she blamed my mom. But the logo on the envelope told us it came from our local pet shop, and we had to follow up on our only lead.

THE LOGO'S A MATCH, BUT FRAN COULD BE DOING ALL THIS TO MAKE ME LOOK SILLY TO GET BACK AT MY MOM.

MAYBE SO, BUT YOU NEED TO FOCUS ON WHAT'S IN FRONT OF YOU, MAX. I THINK THAT'S BASHER INSIDE.

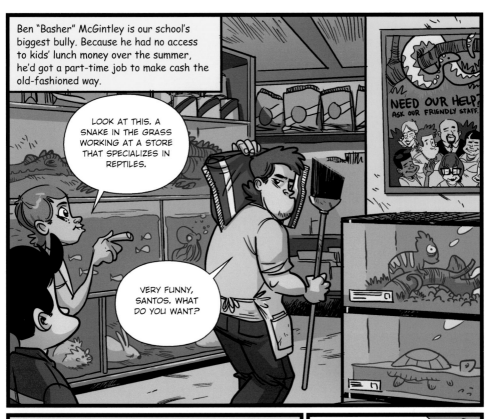

Ben "Basher" McGintley is our school's biggest bully. Because he had no access to kids' lunch money over the summer, he'd got a part-time job to make cash the old-fashioned way.

LOOK AT THIS. A SNAKE IN THE GRASS WORKING AT A STORE THAT SPECIALIZES IN REPTILES.

VERY FUNNY, SANTOS. WHAT DO YOU WANT?

NEED OUR HELP?
ASK OUR FRIENDLY STAFF.

We told Basher about the ad and the envelope, but it didn't seem like he was in a helping mood. So I pulled one of the oldest tricks in the detective book.

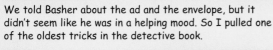

I DON'T KNOW, ALISON. THERE'S NO WAY BASHER'S SMART ENOUGH TO PULL ANY OF THIS OFF.

SURE I AM! MAYBE IT *IS* ME WHO'S MESSING WITH YOU!

WHOA, WHOA, WHOA. WHAT I MEAN IS, I *COULD* PULL IT OFF, BUT IT'S NOT ME.

YOU SHOULD FIND COURTNEY LEGUIN. SHE WAS IN HERE THE OTHER DAY SAYING SHE HATES THE WAY YOU'RE ALWAYS NOSING AROUND. MY CO-WORKER TOLD ME SHE HANGS AROUND THE COMMUNITY POOL.

Courtney LeGuin is a classmate at Central Meadows. During the school year, we had busted her on a case. With time ticking away, we raced to the pool and looked for her, but she was nowhere to be found.

EXCUSE ME. HAVE YOU SEEN THIS GIRL?

UH...

I'VE SEEN HER.

NO LIFEGUARD ON DUTY. SWIM AT YOUR OWN RISK!

The mystery voice belonged to Jake Granger. He goes to our school, likes magic, and thinks he's a detective, too. Apparently, he also thought he was a lifeguard.

OKAY, JAKE. WHERE'S COURTNEY?

NICE TO SEE YOU, TOO. ACTUALLY, I HAVEN'T SEEN HER SINCE LAST WEEK, WHEN SHE SAID SHE WAS PLANNING SOMETHING BIG.

SORRY, I'D LOVE TO STAY AND CHAT, GUYS. BUT I HAVE TO GO. MY SHIFT ENDS AT 2:00.

Time was almost up! We hightailed it to the museum and found the building packed when we arrived just a few minutes after 2:00.

HURRY, MAX. WE'RE ALREADY LATE!

IT'S OKAY, ALISON. THE THINMAN IS 2,000 YEARS OLD. HE CAN'T JUST GET UP AND WALK AWAY.

OH NO! WE'RE TOO LATE! IT'S ALREADY BEEN STOLEN.

THERE YOU ARE, MAX! SOME KID TIPPED ME OFF THAT YOU'D BE HERE. HE SAID YOU HAD A BIG STORY TO BREAK.

I...

...DON'T. BUT I DO KNOW WHO'S MESSING WITH ME. AND WHERE THE MUMMY IS.

Do you know who stole the mummy? All the clues are here. Turn the page for the solution.

THE CASE OF THE...
PUZZLING PUPPET MASTER

Who stole the Thinman Mummy?

No one. The mummy was never stolen. Jake Granger knew the mummy would be out of the museum and sent Max on a wild-goose chase to prove that he had the best mind for mysteries.

Where was the mummy?

The newspaper on the couch in Max's living room said it was out for regular cleaning, so Max knew the mummy was safe the whole time. That's why he didn't tell Fran that the mummy had been stolen when she asked if he had a story to break.

Clues

• On the wall at the Scales 'n' Tails pet shop, Max spotted a poster featuring the staff. It included Basher...and Jake Granger. That explains how Jake got his hands on a Scales 'n' Tails envelope.

• Basher said one of his co-workers told him Courtney hangs out at the community pool. It was Jake. That's how Jake knew Max would go there.

• Max noticed a "No Lifeguard on Duty. Swim at Your Own Risk" sign on the lifeguard chair at the community pool. This proves that Jake wasn't working at the pool. He was there to keep Max on his wild-goose chase.

• Fran said "he" when referring to the person who called and tipped her off. This means it was a boy doing the masterminding.

• While Alison was looking at the empty mummy case, Max was looking around the museum. He noticed someone peeking out from behind a pillar. It was Jake. He wanted to be there to witness Max take the bait and make a fool of himself.

Conclusion

When Max pulled Jake out from behind the pillar and presented his evidence, Jake confessed to trying to set him up. Jake apologized, but Max told him there was no need—he'd had too much fun catching him!

FORENSICS
CORNER

with host
Zoe Palgrave

FINGERPRINTING

WHY?

While a fingerprint alone isn't enough to put you on the trail of the right suspect, it can sure help. Nobody in the world has the same fingerprints as another person, so if you can match prints to a suspect, you increase your chances of solving your case!

HOW?

Practice on yourself:

1. Rub a pencil on a sheet of paper until you have a big, thick pencil mark.

2. Rub your fingertip in the pencil mark until it's fully covered in graphite.

3. Press your covered fingertip onto a piece of clear tape.

4. Stick the tape onto a piece of white paper.

5. Examine your print!

TYPES OF PRINTS

Loops

Whorls

Arches

HINT: Use a magnifying glass to check out the print.

PUT YOUR SKILLS TO THE TEST:

1. Prepare your list of suspects: Have your friends and family members give you their fingerprints by pressing their fingertips onto a washable ink pad and then onto a piece of paper. Label each person's prints.

2. Have one friend or family member volunteer to make clear prints on a smooth, flat surface. Make sure you're not in the room when the person volunteers so you don't know who made the prints and can really test your skills.

3. Select contrasting powder to dust the print. If you have a dark surface, choose white baby powder; if you have a light surface, use some more graphite from a pencil.

4. Using a soft paintbrush or old makeup brush, very gently apply the powder to the fingerprints.

5. Press a piece of clear tape onto the fingerprint, and then peel the tape off carefully.

6. Stick the tape onto a contrasting piece of paper—light powder, dark paper; dark powder, light paper.

7. Compare the print to the prints of your suspects! Whose is it?

WHAT'S IN YOUR KIT?

- ○ Pencil
- ○ Emery board or sandpaper
- ○ Baby powder
- ○ Clear tape
- ○ Black and white paper
- ○ Soft paintbrush
- ○ Washable ink pad

HINT: Have the volunteer run their fingers through their hair or grab a handful of potato chips before they make the print. An oily finger makes a clearer print!

HINT: Collect graphite shavings by rubbing a pencil with an emery board or sandpaper over a piece of paper or paper cup.

DNA COLLECTION

WHY?

DNA, or deoxyribonucleic acid, can tell forensic analysts a lot about whoever or whatever it belongs to—a dog, a monkey, a human, or even...a banana. A stray hair at a crime scene, when collected and analyzed, can tell scientists a lot about who it came from and what that person's role might have been in the crime. Doing this kind of DNA analysis isn't really possible with DIY forensics, but you can practice some similar skills at home.

WHAT'S IN YOUR KIT?

O 1/3 of a ripe banana, peeled

O 150 mL (5/8 cup) distilled or bottled water (not tap water)

O 1 mL (1/4 tsp.) salt

O 5 mL (1 tsp.) baking soda

O 5 mL (1 tsp.) shampoo

O About 50 mL (1/4 cup) rubbing alcohol

O Bowl

O 3 clear drinking glasses

O Metal spoon

O Paper coffee filter

O Wooden stir stick

HOW?

1. Place the banana in a bowl. Add about 25 mL (1/8 cup) of water. Mush up the banana with the water until it's almost smooth (the texture of lumpy cake batter).

2. Pour about 125 mL (1/2 cup) of water into one clear drinking glass. Add the salt, baking soda, and shampoo, and stir it all up.

3. Combine 10 mL (2 tsp.) of the banana mush and 20 mL (4 tsp.) of the mixture from the drinking glass in a new glass. Using a metal spoon, stir for 2 minutes.

4. Strain the whole mixture through a coffee filter into a third clear drinking glass.

5. Measure how much of the mixture you have in your glass, and add an equal amount of rubbing alcohol. Don't mix the two substances—just let them sit for 1 minute.

6. Slip the wooden stick into the fluffy white layer that will form between the layers of the two substances. This is the DNA you're collecting! Slide the DNA up the side of the glass with the stick and lay the covered stick across the top of the glass to dry.

7. Check out your banana DNA sample!

CHROMATOGRAPHY

WHAT'S IN YOUR KIT?

○ Washable black felt-tip markers (different brands or styles)

○ Paper coffee filters cut into strips

○ Glass of water

WHY?

If one of your clues is a written note, it could help to know who wrote it. What if you could test the ink on the note with the pen or marker one of your suspects is carrying? You could narrow down your list of possible culprits by practicing this at-home chromatography. Chromatography is the study of the various colors that a substance is made of. When you test a substance, like ink, in a particular way, you can find out which colors and how much of each color make up the substance.

HINT: Use water-soluble (washable) felt-tip markers because they'll separate into their various colors using only water. Other inks require special solvents to analyze.

HOW?

1. Cut up several strips of coffee-filter paper—one for each marker you have collected.
2. Make a dot with the first marker on the first strip of paper. Label the strip at the opposite end of the dot with the name of the marker that you used. Repeat this step for each marker.
3. One at a time, dip each dotted strip into a glass of water. Be careful not to dip the dot itself into the water—dip the strip just up to the dot. The water will travel up the paper, passing through the dot, and then the colors that make up the black ink will start to separate from each other.
4. Compare the color breakdowns of the strips.

PUT YOUR SKILLS TO THE TEST:

1. Have a few friends each take a different black marker and write a couple of lines on a slip of coffee filter. Cover your eyes so you don't see who wrote with which marker.
2. Test each strip according to step 3 on the left.
3. Compare the notes to the strips you tested earlier—the ones you labeled. Can you figure out who wrote with which marker on which strip of paper?

WALL

NAME: LIAM O'DONNELL
@CREATOR

ACTIVITIES AND INTERESTS:
PLAYING VIDEO GAMES, READING, AND WRITING BOOKS AND GRAPHIC NOVELS. VISIT HIM AT WWW.LIAMODONNELL.COM.

NAME: CRAIG BATTLE
@WRITER

ACTIVITIES AND INTERESTS:
PLAYING BASKETBALL, READING DETECTIVE STORIES, AND OF COURSE, HIDING CLUES IN MAX FINDER COMICS!

NAME: RAMÓN PÉREZ
@ILLUSTRATOR

ACTIVITIES AND INTERESTS:
ILLUSTRATING MAX FINDER COMICS AND DRAWING FOR OTHER BOOKS, GRAPHIC NOVELS, COMICS, MAGAZINES, AND WHATEVER ELSE INTRIGUES HIM.

Easy Ways to Use Max Finder in the Classroom

Want to go beyond the mystery on the page? There are all sorts of fun challenges and ways to read the Max Finder mysteries beyond just discovering a story's culprit. Every comic is loaded with lessons on character, mystery writing, graphic novel structure, and more. Here are a few pointers to help set you off in the right direction.

Genre Study:

What makes a mystery? Students can work in groups to research the elements of mysteries—clues, suspects, detectives, red herrings—and present their findings to the rest of the class.

Classroom connections: language arts, media literacy

DIY Mystery:

Using the guide in Volume 3, students can write and illustrate their own mini-mystery, then trade with a partner and try to solve someone else's creation.

Classroom connections: language arts, media literacy, visual arts

Character Study:

Have students study the roles (bully, snitch, prankster) that Max Finder characters play over a number of the comics and graph the results. Is there a pattern?

Classroom connections: math, language arts, media literacy

Comic Format Study:

What makes a comic? Students can work in groups to research the conventions of comics—speech bubbles, caption boxes, paneled illustrations—and present their findings to the rest of the class.

Classroom connections: language arts, media literacy

SOLVE A *MAX FINDER MYSTERY* EVERY MONTH IN *OWL MAGAZINE.*

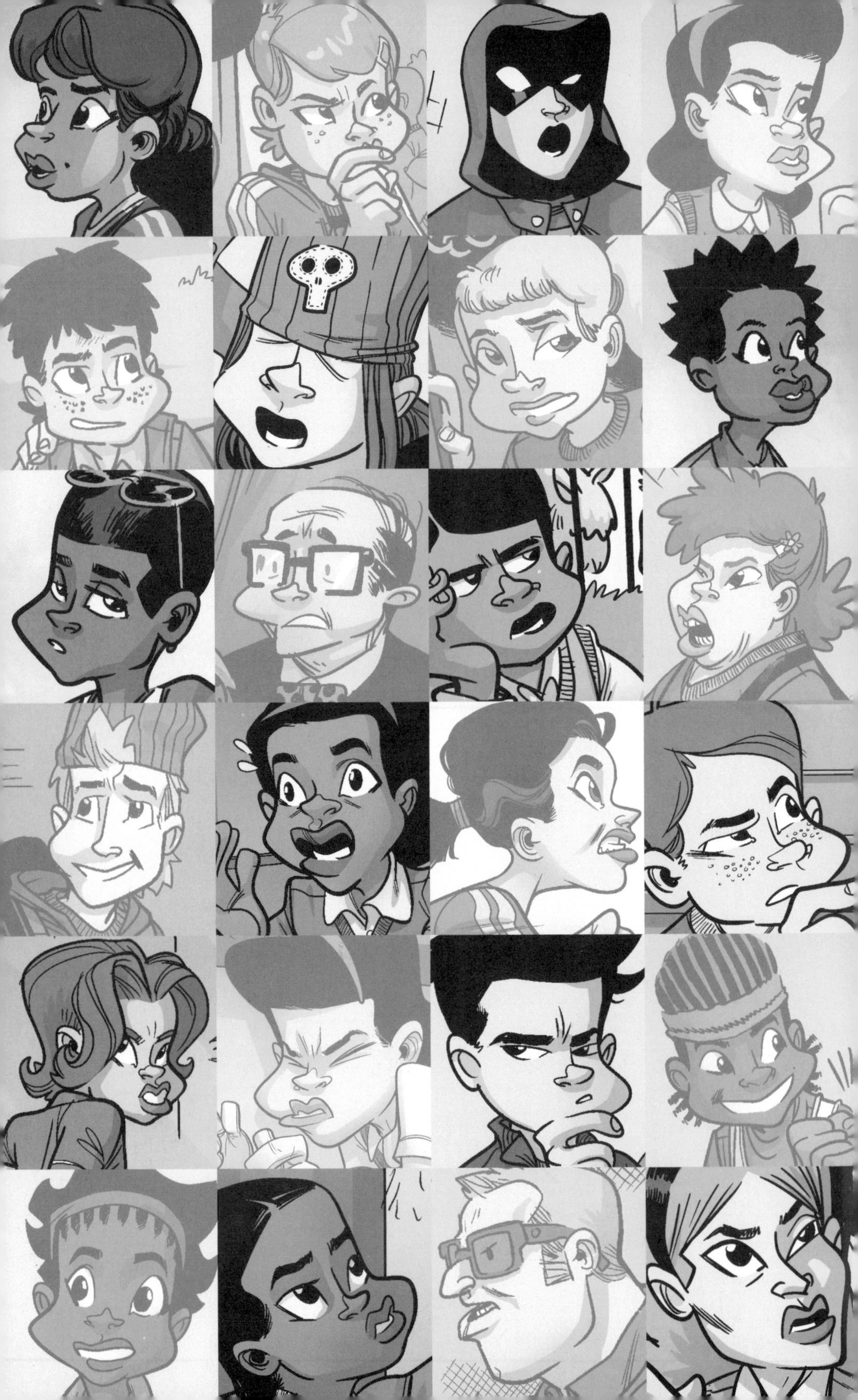